Olori

Eturuvie Erebor

A DOZ Chronicles Romance Series

ISBN: 978-1-8383844-4-9

OLORI

Published in London, England by Eturuvie Erebor trading as DOZ Chronicles, a unit of DOZ Network.

Destined to be queen. Doomed to love another. Will fate prevail?

Amenze wants to be married like her friends, but she is not so desperate that she will settle for the King of Warri Kingdom, who is older than her father! Fully intent on fleeing the prophecy that she is destined to be the Olori of the Warri Kingdom, Amenze returns to London to live a little and walk on the wild side. She crosses paths a second time with the charming but elusive Bawo Domingo. Can she escape the prophecy, or is she bound to fulfil it?

Bawo is a handsome man capable of capturing any woman's heart. His charms are alluring, but his indecision and fickle flirtation still leave something to be desired. Despite his hesitancy, Bawo cannot help but find Amenze beautiful and irresistible. Sparks fly, igniting a whirlwind romance that further complicates her plans. But he has secrets of his own that could change her fate for good.

Dear Reader,

This book has been in the works for three years, and I can finally bring it to you. My connection to the Warri Kingdom through my paternal grandmother, Ayenor Buwa, made me fall in love with this story even before I put pen to paper (or fingers to keyboard). She was the daughter of Chief Buwa Beru, the Eyinmosan of Warri Kingdom, who coincidentally crowned Olu Erejuwa II. As a child, I remember watching the coronation of Olu Atuwatse II. The boat regatta was breathtakingly beautiful. I am proud of my Itsekiri heritage and hope I have done justice to the culture with this book. Hopefully, my dad would be proud of what I have done here.

The story is as dear to my heart as the Itsekiri people and culture. As a romantic, I enjoy immersing myself in the world of a captivating romance novel, either through reading or writing. I love the stories I have shared with you so far and those that will follow. But Amenze and Bawo's story will always have a special place in my heart.

Thank you for being patient with me as I finished my bar exams and returned to the art of storytelling to finish this incredible love story. Here it is, finally. I hope you enjoy it.

Remember, you can write to me through my website, www.eturuvieerebor.com, or via my email eturuvie@eturuvieerebor.com.

I look forward to hearing from you.

Evie.

For my mother, Eyitemi

and

my father, Owumi

Special thanks to Miss Toritseju G. Ebiareneyin

PROLOGUE

Oma Domingo heaved a sigh of relief as the lights of the ancient town came into focus.

Ode Itsekiri, the ancestral home of all Itsekiri sons and daughters. She smiled despite the sharp pains coursing through her body. She was finally here; finally home.

"*Mo dokpe.* Thank you very much," she mumbled to the man paddling the canoe as he helped her out of the small boat and onto the wooden deck on the riverbank. She wrapped the Ankara cloth she had draped around herself more tightly as she made her way one step at a time, ignoring the pain, determined to reach her sister's home on time.

Her sister, Alero Domingo, fondly called Sisi Alero or Sisi Domingo by all who knew her, had been widowed many years ago and had never had a child. She was a traditional midwife who had delivered many children in the community. Many were now established men and women who often returned to pay homage with gifts, enabling Sisi Domingo to own her small two-bedroom home in Ode Itsekiri.

The Domingo family gained fame among the Itsekiri people for introducing them to the Portuguese. More than a hundred years ago, one of their forebears spotted the Portuguese as they arrived in Ode Itsekiri and welcomed them into his home. This led to marriage with the Portuguese and the adoption of the Portuguese name Domingo. They were not only Itsekiris but also Portuguese, maintaining their relations to this day.

They were a big family, but not a close-knit one. Their late father was the parent of many children, while their mother only had Alero and Oma. The sisters shared a close bond despite the twenty-five-year age gap between them. Oma did not know their mother, as she passed away before Oma's first birthday, and Sisi Alero raised Oma as her daughter.

Sisi Alero displayed a strong sense of protectiveness towards Oma, and it took considerable persuasion before she consented to her living and working in Warri because of the decreasing availability of jobs in Ode Itsekiri. That was four years ago when Oma was twenty-one years old. Initially, Oma came home at every opportunity, but for the past nine months, she did not come home, although she did not fail to send Sisi Alero her monthly allowances and write letters about how she fared. A little about how she fared: she did not think Sisi Alero would appreciate the entire story, so she kept some of it to herself.

She let out another sigh, partly to bear the pain she experienced and partly to regain her composure. She had arrived at Sisi Alero's little, two-bedroom, red-brick bungalow, less than a mile from the waterfront. Shortly, she would face her sister, who played the motherly role and shared her wisdom. With a sense of shame, Oma acknowledged that she had not followed her teachings.

Inside, the lights stayed switched on, indicating that Sisi Alero, a woman who followed a routine of going to bed early and waking up early, was still awake. Oma placed her little bag, packed in a hurry and bearing all her most important possessions on the little steps, and after wrapping herself more tightly, she knocked on the door.

"*Eri nesin*? Who is it?" Sisi Alero's shrill but strong voice enquired from within.

Oma smiled despite her discomfort. Yes, that was the Sisi Alero Domingo she was familiar with.

"Sisi, *Emi ren*. It is me, Omasan."

The door swung open instantly. Luckily, it opened inside, sparing her face from a harsh impact. She barely picked up her bag before Sisi Alero enveloped her in a fierce hug.

In pain, she winced, causing the older woman to step back and peer at her with wise eyes that never missed a thing.

"Oma, are you ill?"

Tears welled up in Oma's eyes. Tears of relief, knowing she had returned home and all would be well. Before she said anything, Sisi Alero ushered her into the tidy, pleasant living room. Once inside, Oma put her bag down and turned to face her sister, removing the wrapper she had used to cover herself. As she did, Sisi's eyes widened in shock.

"Sisi, please forgive me. I have no one else to turn to and nowhere to go!" Oma cried.

"Oh, Oma!" Sisi covered her mouth with her calloused hands. "Oma, you are pregnant! How could you?!"

"I am sorry," was all she managed to utter before another surge of pain spread through her body, forcing her to double over and clutch her abdomen. Then, as it subsided, came the sensation of needing to relieve her bowels. "Sisi, please, I need to use the toilet," she announced, overwhelmed by the irresistible urge to push.

"No! You are in labour." Sisi Alero took her arm and led her into the small room that used to be hers until she went to live and work in Warri.

And so began the longest night of Oma Domingo's life. She pushed and pushed and pushed and pushed, and finally, in the wee hours of the morning, a woman about Sisi Alero's age and a traditional midwife in Ode Itsekiri placed the tiny baby in her arms.

Oma was weary, but not too exhausted to admire her beautiful baby. As she looked at him, her smile expressed triumph. It proved to be worthwhile in the end. The entire experience had been worth it; one day, her name would be known by all Itsekiri people. She looked at the midwife, then at Sisi Alero, who wept softly, and finally at the sleeping baby in her arms.

"*Onetoritsebawoete!*" she proclaimed and closed her eyes.

CHAPTER ONE

The Kingdom of Benin …. Today

Amenze concluded that her life, as she had known it, was officially finished. She observed with great interest and a slight pang of sadness as her dear childhood friend Tiyan Alile was seated on her fiancé's lap. Traditionally, this meant they were now man and wife. Tiyan was now officially Mrs Usi Isekhure, the wife of the Chief Priest of the Benin Kingdom. First, Eki, then Ede and now Tiyan. Amenze's friends were now married, and her relationship with them would change regardless of whether she wanted it to. Their friendship would take on a different disposition.

Amenze sighed in resignation. Despite being practical and realistic, witnessing the joy of her married friends made her feel like she was missing out on something special. She secretly desired that something special for herself. Yes. She desired to understand the essence of falling in love. She wished to be married to a man she loved and have her belly swell with his baby!

Amenze considered her relationship with Dimitris Papadopoulos and bit back a groan. It frustrated her that her relationship with Dimitris Papadopoulos was going nowhere fast. Seeing her friends marry and get pregnant left her completely dissatisfied with her life and also led to a subtle resentment for her boyfriend and the desire to bring the relationship to an end. She envied her friends.

She wasn't the only person who noticed that her friends were entering into matrimony. Her mother noticed, and on the eve of another friend's wedding ceremony, Tuedor Giwa-Amu called her only daughter to the living room for a chat. She thought Amenze was a fool for wanting to break up with Dimitris instead of using her feminine wiles to get him to marry her.

Amenze was a realist. Dating Dimitris Papadopoulos had been fun, but she didn't think they had what Eki and Oba Osad or Tiyan and Usi had. Or even what Ede and Sato had. If they did, they would get married, not constantly seek the latest Michelin-starred restaurant to try for dinner. She'd become fed up with that! Love, romance, and marriage were what she desired. Her desire was to be looked at with the same intensity as Oba Osad looked at Eki, as Usi looked at Tiyan, and as Sato looked at Ede. Oh, and even as her father looked at her mother after almost forty years of marriage!

"Don't you love him?" her mother had asked during their little chat last night, a puzzled expression on her ageing but still beautiful face.

"Love?" Amenze snorted. "Of course not."

"I will never understand you."

"That makes you and most people," Amenze had murmured. And me, she'd added silently.

Amenze's scowl deepened as she recollected her mother's nagging. Her mother thought she was getting old and reminded her that she had already been married at Amenze's age.

As midnight approached, Amenze decided to say her goodbyes and leave the party. Tiyan, the glowing bride, had been escorted to her husband's home according to the Benin native law and customs. The lavish reception at the groom's house was now quickly ending, with guests leaving one after the other as the early hours of the following day approached.

The night was as pretty as a picture, with the moon as a backdrop. But it was both warm and humid. Amenze stepped out of the air-conditioned three-storey house, instantly hot and uncomfortable in her bridesmaid outfit - a red long-sleeve mermaid dress made of luxurious embroidered fabric. The traditional Benin *Okuku* hairstyle was done beautifully, and her neck was adorned with multiple strings of coral beads, adding to her discomfort. With one hand holding up her floor-length dress, she walked down the cobbled drive, her red stiletto heels clicking against the ground, while palm trees and garden lamps lined the path to the car park.

Amenze had just reached the white Kia Sportage she'd borrowed from her mother when she heard the groom's voice behind her.

"Amenze, just a minute!"

Amenze turned around, and sure enough, Chief Usi Isekhure approached her as she stood in the large open car park outside his vast home. She furrowed her brows as she tried to decipher what he wanted.

"Hey, Amenze. I've been meaning to have a quick word with you all day." His smile was quickly replaced with a frown.

Amenze disliked his intent gaze. Had she done something wrong, broken some traditional or cultural protocol, perhaps? Chief Usi Isekhure wasn't just her best friend's husband; he was the revered Chief Priest of the Benin Kingdom, and as the mouthpiece of the gods of the land—his word was potent.

He was not a man to be taken lightly. Her heart beat a little faster as the frown on Usi's face deepened, and he came closer. She wasn't great friends with Usi, not being present while his romance with Tiyan blossomed. But he seemed laid back the few times she'd seen or been around him, causing her to wonder, *what now?*

"What is the matter, Usi?" Amenze wondered whether it was a good time to be on a first-name basis with him. The man standing before her didn't look like a friend, but rather like a chief priest.

Usi did not respond to her question. Instead, he caught her chin and slowly and carefully scrutinised her face.

"There is no mistake. You are the Olori of the Warri Kingdom. A Benin woman born for the Warri throne. He placed the crown on your head and called you Olori Sisan." Usi released her chin.

Amenze did not burst out laughing for three reasons. No one dared laugh at the Chief Priest of the Benin Kingdom. Chief Priest Isekhure had never been wrong. Hadn't she witnessed how Eki tried to escape the prophecy only to run right into it? Her heart raced even faster.

The third reason she didn't laugh was that her middle name was Sisan. It was an Itsekiri name given to her by her Itsekiri mother but rarely ever used. Apart from Eki and Tiyan, no one outside her family knew her name was Sisan. Unless Tiyan told him. But why would Tiyan mention her rarely used name to Usi?

Then she pondered Usi's use of the title Olori. Olori was the title used by the queen of the Warri kingdom. Was she going to be a queen? Queen of the Warri Kingdom? Who had Usi seen placing the crown on her head? She presumed the words were thoughts in her heart until she heard Usi answer.

"The Olu of Warri!"

Amenze gasped. *The Olu of Warri? Olu Ginuwa III?* At seventy-one years of age, the man was *older* than her father!

"Olu Ginuwa III?" she demanded angrily.

"Do nothing to mess this up. Do not attempt to make it happen," Usi warned severely before walking away.

Do not attempt to make it happen?! What did that mean? Amenze thought with chagrin as she entered her car and slammed the door shut. She had no intention of trying to make the ludicrous prophecy happen! Why would she want to make a marriage to a man older than her father happen? If anything, she planned to do the exact opposite and do everything she could to make it *not* happen!

As she drove home, in a foul mood, she cursed her rotten luck. What was the deal with her? Why did she always get the short end of the stick? Eki married the young and handsome Oba of Benin, and Tiyan married the young and handsome Chief Priest of the Benin kingdom. Ede married the young and handsome bodyguard of the king. They all married *young* and *handsome husbands.*

And who would she marry? The old, ugly, never mind polygamous Olu of Warri. She punched the steering wheel and wanted to scream out her frustration! The gods were most unkind to her. Fate was most unkind to her. Life was cruel to her! She refused to accept this without a fight. She would go to great lengths to make it not happen, and in the end, if it still happened, well, at least she would not be going to the old man with her virginity intact. Note to self: Amenze, get rid of virginity as soon as you return to London.

"You look like you're returning from a funeral instead of a wedding," her mother commented as soon as Amenze entered the living room.

Amenze's mother was an average-height woman with a well-rounded body gained through childbirth and years of cooking and eating sumptuous meals. She had a charming face that suited her plus-size body and was fashionable, always wearing clothes that flattered her figure.

Tonight, she dressed casually in Ankara palazzo pants and a denim shirt. She was a proud Itsekiri woman from the Warri kingdom, addressed fondly as Sisi Tuedor or Sisi Giwa-Amu. She loathed being called "mama" or "aunty" as it made her feel too old at sixty. Older Itsekiri women shared this sentiment and were addressed as Sisi.

Amenze wasn't surprised to see her mother still awake. Sisi Tuedor would stay up whenever any family member was out late. She had done it for her husband and sons when they lived at home and began going out with friends at night. Now, she did it for her only daughter and last child.

Amenze dropped onto the deliciously soft leather sofa beside her mother and kicked off her stilettoes. "It seemed like a funeral at the end."

Her mother looked baffled. "Did anything go wrong? Are Tiyan and her husband okay?"

"They are fine, Mum. Nothing wrong at their end, but plenty at mine."

Sisi Tuedor knitted her brows. "Tell me what happened," she invited, her frown deepening as Amenze recounted her brief meeting with Usi.

"Well, at least now we are certain you will marry!"

"Mummy!"

"Listen to me, my daughter; there are worse things in life than marrying a man much older than you are."

"I don't believe you are saying this, Mum." Amenze shook her head in utter disbelief.

"*Niko wo fe gin demi fo*? What would you have me say, Amenze? Last night, you insisted you wanted to break up with Dimitris, even though I thought you were better off giving your relationship a chance. I told you that getting another man may be challenging and that African women living in the United Kingdom struggle to marry. Some of your father's distant cousins, who travelled to live in the UK years ago, are still unmarried in their forties. I worry about you emulating them, especially as you will be in London for another three years for your doctoral programme. Now, a prophecy foretells your marriage to a king. Should I say the gods forbid because he is much older?"

"Here we go again." Amenze groaned and rolled her eyes. They discussed this yesterday, and Amenze slept late. Perhaps she should go to bed and catch up on much-needed sleep. She rose to her feet. "I'm going to bed, Mum. If I must marry Olu Ginuwa III, then I will, but I will go to him screaming and kicking!"

"Hmm… *Oton mi tse denden*. Child, be careful. The chief priest has warned you not to mess this up; please listen to him. It's better to be married to an older man than to be an older unmarried woman. You are my only daughter; please let your heart pity your mother."

Amenze rolled her eyes as she bent and picked up her shoes. Her mother could be dramatic when the occasion suited her. She'd used the same blackmailing tactics with each one of her three older sons. The blackmail and drama never got old.

Just as Amenze walked away from her mother, her father walked in. "Who is getting married?" he peered through the upper portion of his bifocals, first at his wife and then at his daughter.

At sixty-five years old, Dr Giwa-Amu was a renowned consultant gynaecologist who had delivered many prominent Benin men and women. His private fertility and maternity clinic, Giwa-Amu Clinic, next door to their residence, was the foremost private gynaecology clinic in the kingdom. For that reason, the city's authorities named their street Giwa-Amu Crescent.

Her parents were very different. Amenze frequently wondered why her father married her mother. He was gentle and soft-spoken, and she was the complete opposite.

"No one is getting married, Dad." Amenze walked up to her tired-looking father and kissed his cheek. "Welcome, Dad. How was your day at the clinic?"

"It was good, thank you." He stroked her cheek affectionately as she pulled away. "Are you okay?"

"Yes, I am, just a little tired." Amenze feigned a smile. He looked at her long and hard to show he didn't believe her, but didn't push the matter.

As her father strolled further into the living room and settled himself in his favourite seat, the lazy-boy recliner, he and her mum exchanged mumbled greetings that would make anyone think they had a lovers' tiff, but Amenze understood her parents well enough by now to appreciate this was their standard way of saluting each other. Also, they had seen each other over dinner as her dad made it a habit to take a break and come home to eat lunch and dinner with his wife.

"Dr Giwa-Amu, I am glad you're home. I was just having a chat with Amenze. Both her friends, the Alile girls, are married. Oloi Eki will soon become a mother, while Amenze plans to end her relationship instead of trying to get her boyfriend to propose. She is living in the United Kingdom. Who finds a husband in the UK? You remember your cousins, now in their forties and still unmarried?"

Amenze sighed and quietly left the room. After last night, she wouldn't stick around to hear all of that. Her father could take her place tonight.

"Poor Dad," she mumbled as she climbed the stairs and went to her bedroom. "But better you than me, Dad." She stifled a giggle.

CHAPTER TWO

London, United Kingdom .... Today

"What's going on? Bawo Domingo asked as Dimitris Papadopoulos took out a chair and joined him at his table in the elegant gentlemen's club in Mayfair, where they both held memberships.

He sipped his rum and Coke and signalled the waiter while glancing appreciatively at the beautiful pianist at the polished mahogany grand piano. Her radiant smile, soft voice, and the piano's even softer notes provided a welcome distraction.

Slowly, he brought his attention back to his companion. He wasn't looking forward to this conversation. With the mess that was currently his love life, if it could be called that, he had no moral justification to tell another man how to rule his affairs. And that wasn't all. There was also the girl in question and his brief encounter with her over a year ago. He shifted in his seat. That issue served as a satisfactory cause to avoid bringing up this subject with Dimitris. But with Aphrodite Papadopoulos being so tearful and hysterical only a few days ago, what choice did he have?

Aphrodite, being five years older than Dimitris, took it upon herself to make sure he respected their late father's wishes to marry from the upper echelon of Greek society. Their father handpicked the girl in question, the daughter of his friend and fellow shipping magnate, Elena Mastoroudes, and stated that Dimitris would not fully come into his inheritance until the marriage to Elena happened. Aphrodite was losing her mind because Dimitris was reluctant to officially become engaged to Elena and set a wedding date.

Aphrodite believed that Bawo could convince Dimitris to see reason and terminate his current relationship with a certain girl–someone Aphrodite considered insignificant–and become engaged to Elena. As Aphrodite saw it, and Bawo agreed, Dimitris had spent three years sowing his wild oats, and it was time for him to establish stability and assume full control of the business, which, upon his marriage, would merge with Mastoroudes Shipping.

Bawo would have declined the request to speak to Dimitris if it were anyone else. At twenty-six, he was a grown man, even though Aphrodite liked to perceive him as a boy. He possessed the capability to organise his own life without Bawo's interference, but how could Bawo not interfere? How could he decline Aphrodite's request after everything their father, Aristotle Papadopoulos, did for him? He, who had been no better than a street urchin, sat in this club for the wealthy with a thousand-pound suit on his back and a business worth over a billion pounds because Aristotle gave him a chance and mentored him.

He was strict and demanding of Bawo, but he taught him everything he knew about business and wealth creation. Bawo, driven by a strong desire to break free from poverty, acquired the knowledge, and the outcomes were now evident. He would be eternally grateful to Aristotle, and if supporting Aphrodite by talking to Dimitris was one way to show his gratitude, he would do it.

However, his relationship with Dimitris was strained because the younger man resented that Bawo had been to Aristotle, a son figure and a protégé. The resentment increased as Bawo lived up to Aristotle's every expectation of him. Before the older man passed, over three years ago, he held an immense sense of pride in Bawo, who had become a successful entrepreneur.

He angled his head to study Dimitris, making eye contact with the man seven years younger than his thirty-three years.

"Aphrodite called me two days ago. She was hysterical. So, tell me, what's going on?"

Dimitris's eyes lit up with rage as Bawo maintained eye contact, and he calmly observed the younger man attempting to control himself.

"I told Aphrodite that your love life is none of my business, but she insisted I owed it to Aristotle to speak to you. Hence, I summoned you." Bawo looked away again toward the pianist. She looked at him and smiled. He winked and watched with satisfaction as she turned red.

"Well, you are right on that account. It is none of your business how I choose to conduct my personal life. And you're in no position to lecture me, not with the scandal you've been through recently." Dimitris clenched and unclenched the hand resting on the sturdy oak circular table.

Bawo laughed. That was a low blow and reasonably expected of Dimitris. He would not take offence. What he did, he did for Aristotle. Even if Dimitris chose not to listen to him, he would leave this meeting satisfied he had done something for Aristotle. Besides, if Dimitris focused on the scandal perhaps, he would not suspect an agenda. Bawo instantly rebuked himself. Did he have a hidden agenda?

"Aphrodite believes your current relationship makes you drag your feet where Elena is concerned. Consider how your actions will affect Elena, her father, and the proposed merger." He paused as the waiter appeared at their table, and Dimitris ordered a drink.

"Yes, I am with Amenze. You must remember her. You met her once. We're still together," Dimitris announced as the waiter walked away.

Betraying no emotion, Bawo turned to glance at Dimitris. "You've been with her for over a year now. It sounds serious. Is it serious? I ask because when you were told to go and sow your wild oats before settling down with Elena, the idea was not to stay with one woman for almost two years."

"Eighteen months." Dimitris shrugged. "It's not serious enough that I would marry her. I realise I must return to Elena, eventually. But we're happy together. She loves me. How can I break her heart?"

He locked eyes with Bawo. There was triumph somewhere in the brown depths.

Bawo held the gaze briefly, giving nothing away through his expression. "I would be surprised if she didn't," he muttered dryly, lifting his glass to his lips. "I am no expert on love, but I know this: love doesn't pay the bills. It won't keep you in the style to which you're accustomed. What will, however, is getting your full inheritance and merging the business with Mastoroudes Shipping. And neither will happen while you're stalling where Elena's concerned."

"I know that!" Dimitris snapped as he accepted his gin and tonic from the waiter and took a sip before bringing the glass down hard on the table. "I don't see what the issue is. I try to spend time with Elena in Greece, and I haven't said or done anything to suggest that I won't marry her."

Bawo stared at him long and hard. "I beg to differ. You may have said nothing to suggest you won't marry her. But the longer you stay with this girl of yours and don't officially propose to Elena, the more you suggest to her through your actions that you might have second thoughts."

Dimitris scoffed. "That's ridiculous!"

Bawo leaned back in his chair and shrugged. "Perhaps. And I am no expert in women's behaviour. But I think Aphrodite's hysterical phone call suffices to suggest something is wrong. When last did you see Elena? When last did you see her father?"

"I don't know. Perhaps three months ago. I have been busy, okay?"

Bawo nodded. "I have no problems with your busyness. Elena might, and if she does, her father will. If he does, he may wonder if he shouldn't alter the agreement with your father. Elena is a beautiful girl with a sizeable dowry. Any man would happily marry her."

Dimitris became motionless and gazed at Bawo. "What are you saying? Mastoroudes had a deal with my father."

"Yes, he did. But you are not upholding your part of the deal; why should he uphold his?" Bawo quizzed.

"Did Aphrodite say—"

"Aphrodite said nothing of the sort, but I wonder why she asked me to intervene and why she was upset and distraught."

"Aphrodite's always been a passionate woman, a real drama queen."

"You want to bet your inheritance and the merger on that?" Bawo held the younger man's gaze. As Dimitris's shoulders slumped, he shook his head and picked up his drink. "I thought not."

He sipped his drink and waited for Dimitris to speak, but the other man seemed to have lost his tongue.

"My advice: get rid of your girl, get down to Greece, and make things right with Elena and her father." As Dimitris hesitated, Bawo leaned forward, placing a long, well-manicured hand on the table. "Do you have something you're not telling me? Is there a reason you can't end this relationship? Is she pregnant?"

"No!" Dimitris looked scandalised. "I wouldn't be that careless."

"You've been with her only this entire time?"

Dimitris looked uncomfortable and quickly glanced around him. Then he leaned across the table. "No," he admitted in a voice slightly above a whisper. "There've been others, but I've been discreet!"

"I see. So, it's possible that we're not too different then, you and me." Bawo taunted before he could stop himself.

As Dimitris opened his mouth to retort, Bawo held up his hand. "Please hear me out. If you haven't been faithful to her, she can't be that important to you, and you can't be too concerned about breaking her heart. Wrap up the affair ASAP and fix a date for your wedding with Elena."

"Seeing as you're a master of loving and leaving them, advise me on how to do it." It was sarcasm, but Bawo took the bait, regardless.

"Give her jewellery or something expensive as a parting gift. It works every time. Trust me."

Dimitris snorted. "Amenze is not that type of girl. She's not a gold digger. She's a decent girl, the kind you take home to your mother."

"Whatever, Dimitris," Bawo dismissed with a careless wave of the hand, possibly because he preferred not to think about her meeting Dimitris' mother. "You won't be taking her home to your mother, so wrap this up. Elena is waiting, and so is her father. The longer you keep her waiting, the more pissed he'll get."

"I've got to go; your shadow's here," Dimitris sneered as he lifted his glass to drain the contents. Bawo glanced towards the doorway and witnessed the entrance of his friend Sufyani Boateng.

He had been acquainted with Suf for a period exceeding ten years. Besides serving as his lawyer, Suf was his best friend and brother-in-arms. They acquired and managed numerous businesses under the House of Oma label. Suf got huge payments from each deal, making him very wealthy. They were working on a merger deal with an African king, Obi Chez Aboh, and if all went well, they would be even richer. Suf texted him an hour ago, citing the deal as a reason to speak to him urgently, and he'd asked him to meet him up at the club, hoping to have enough time to talk first to Dimitris.

Bawo rose to his feet as Dimitris rose to leave. "Thanks for meeting me. And remember what I said." They shook hands. Bawo slapped Dimitris slightly on the back and turned to watch Suf as Dimitris walked away.

Both men shook hands and sat down. "What was that about? Why did the kid look grumpy?"

Bawo chuckled at Suf's reference to Dimitris as a kid. But he supposed that as Suf was thirty-six, he could rightly refer to Dimitris as such.

"I gave him some advice about his love life."

Suf instantly cringed. "My brother, you should advise nobody about their love life. For starters, you know nothing about love."

Bawo grinned, revealing perfect white and straight teeth. "You'll be surprised that I know enough to advise Dimitris."

Suf shook his head, still looking horrified. "Well, whatever the advice you gave him, it can't be any good. I hope he didn't take it."

"It's still too early to tell." Bawo beckoned to the waiter. "What do you need to discuss that couldn't wait until tomorrow?"

Suf leaned across the table and studied Bawo with grim eyes. "I have bad news. Your earlier problems have not dissipated, so you won't go to Lagos tomorrow. I will attend the meeting with Aboh. I'll also be taking the jet."

Bawo scowled, irritated at being issued orders. "I do not appreciate your tone, Sufyani. What problems haven't gone away? I have a meeting with Chez Aboh tomorrow."

The server appeared at their table just then, and both men paused their conversation. Suf ordered a Vodka Soda, and Bawo ordered another rum and Coke.

As the waiter left, Suf turned to Bawo with a slight shake of his head. "*I have a meeting with Chez Aboh tomorrow.*"

Bawo eyed him calmly. "Care to explain yourself?"

Suf needed no further encouragement. He powered up his iPad and passed it across. Bawo reached for it with a steady hand, but his heart raced.

What now? He wondered.

Bawo's scowl deepened as he peered at the device's screen. He recognised the online magazine and was familiar with the story, although he never read it when it was published. He did not read trash. The incident happened about six months ago and was one huge misunderstanding.

A woman who frequented his London spa was interrupted during a massage by paparazzi. She ran, covered by a small towel, and collided with him as he exited his office. He grabbed her and the towel to steady her and keep her modest. The paparazzi took pictures and fled before his security intervened. The images were published the same day and made the news—trash news.

The woman, a stunning mixed-race model often followed by the paparazzi, was engaged to Oba Akran of Lagos. Oba Akran instantly broke off the engagement, and everyone blamed Bawo.

Bawo tried at the time to understand why she fled from the paparazzi. Perhaps, as the fiancée of an African king who upheld old-fashioned customs, receiving a massage from a man would be disapproved of. But if she ran for that reason, she only complicated matters because she bumped into Bawo, and the photo that followed convinced many they were lovers.

His PR team attempted to do some damage control, but the story, like his partying playboy reputation, would not quickly disappear. He dismissed it as lies that no sane person would read, let alone believe.

"I have just discovered that Obi Chez Aboh and Oba Akran, being African royal fathers and council members, are great friends. But that's not all."

"There's more?" Bawo placed the iPad on the table and paid attention to the waiter who had arrived with their drinks.

"Yes. There's more." Suf took a long sip of his Vodka Soda. "Akran has considerable shares in Hotel Chez Terez. And he is on a personal mission to hurt you. Aboh is trying to be cautious."

"Is this why you are here? You know what happened, Suf. This is garbage."

Bawo wondered if he was about to lose a lucrative deal to a story built on falsehood. Obi Chez Aboh was a well-established businessman with a chain of luxury hotels in every major African city. Bawo wanted to establish his spas in those hotels to take his business beyond Europe.

Aboh had been delighted with the proposal, convinced that Bawo's top-notch spas were precisely what his business required to advance to the next stage and penetrate the European market, where the House of Oma held sway, be it in the realm of spas or high-end products for women.

Was Aboh now reluctant to proceed because of a stupid story in some trashy celebrity gossip magazine that targeted wealthy Africans in the diaspora, smearing their reputations?

Suf leaned closer. "Listen, Bawo, it's not just this story or whether you slept with Akran's woman. Your playboy reputation precedes you, and key stakeholders in this deal have reason to believe you're unstable and, therefore, unreliable."

"Carry on," Bawo encouraged, confident there was more.

"Chez Aboh called today, considering withdrawing from the deal due to concerns about your instability and lack of morals. Also, as this meeting is in Lagos, I expect Akran will be present. If you show up, you can kiss the deal goodbye."

Bawo shifted in his armchair, prompting Suf to lean across the table.

"I propose I meet with Aboh, or Aboh and Akran, and discuss the deal and the benefit to Hotel Chez Terez. Hopefully, he will change his mind. But I suggest you remain in London and keep a low profile over the next few weeks, if possible."

Despite his bruised ego, Bawo ignored his snide remark and admitted that Suf was right.

"You know what else will be helpful? You getting married."

"It will not happen. I have no plans to attach myself to a ball and chain," Bawo countered, letting his eyes travel toward the beautiful pianist again and blowing her a kiss as their eyes met.

Suf threw up his hands in exasperation. "Bawo, as your friend, lawyer, and business partner on mergers and acquisitions past, present, and future, my advice to you is this: find yourself a wife! You're thirty-three, living life in the fast lane, changing women as often as you change your underwear. You are the embodiment of instability. Most people won't do any major business with you." He paused for a drink and allowed the words to sink in. "You don't have to marry for love. You could get a convenient wife while you continue to fool around. Discreetly, of course."

Bawo studied him. "Is that what you do?"

"Of course not. Zuhrah is the love of my life. I've never cheated on her, and I never will."

Bawo snorted, but Suf ignored him. "All I am saying is that you must get your affairs together for our common business projects if nothing else. And as much as I love you, if your disorderliness affects my reputation and business concerns, I will walk."

Bawo sprung to his feet. "This meeting is over, Suf. You better secure this deal, or you'll be looking for another job. Good night."

CHAPTER THREE

Amenze drank her champagne and let her eyes travel around the large ballroom with its antiquated interior design. The crowd was thinning, but the ball was still in full swing. Couples occupied the dance floor while guests gathered in small groups around the room, engaging in conversation and laughter.

Would it be impolite if she flicked her wrist to steal a quick glance at her watch? She wished Efua would quit mingling and greeting so they could leave. No doubt it must be almost 11 pm now. Amenze longed for her bed. She would go, but she didn't want to displease Efua.

Efua was her flatmate, and Amenze preferred to view her as a friend. This event held a special place in Efua's heart. Her older half-brother, a celebrity rugby player treated for a heart defect a couple of years ago, set up a foundation to help children born with a similar heart defect access the best medical help available. Tonight, the charity debuted in London, although most of its work would be carried out in Africa.

Efua saw it as a place to meet eligible African bachelors. Marriage was foremost on her mind at this stage of her life, and every activity she engaged in, including her nine-to-five, was just a way to meet her future husband and, Amenze thought wryly, quite elusive Mr Right. Elusive because she was twenty-nine and had been actively seeking a spouse for almost half that time, to no avail. She didn't even have a steady boyfriend to show for all her endeavours. So yes, her Mr Right was quite elusive.

Efua thought it would be good for Amenze to network and meet potential Benin investors who could become assets to Elevate, the business she ran with her two friends, Eki and Tiyan. Amenze acknowledged that with the hundreds of people present, most Africans, including a few Benin millionaires living in Europe, this presented an excellent networking opportunity. And more so as Elevate hosted its second pitch event in a few weeks.

She watched with a smile as a prominent international league footballer of Benin origin, Ero Amadasun, looking dashing in a black tux, approached her. She was introduced to him moments after arriving at the party, and he promised to find her later. Well, it seemed he had.

As she conversed with him, she sensed eyes boring holes in her back. Ah yes, that back she'd uncovered.

What had she been thinking?

She had no idea.

She'd gone a little overboard with preparations for this charity ball. Efua asked her to straighten her hair, have her nails done, and get a makeup artist to do her makeup, and she obliged. Wanting to be a tad bit more daring, she chose to wear this black ankle-length tuxedo halter neck dress that left her entire back exposed and featured a slit running up the side, revealing her toned legs when she walked. Her mother, not to mention her two closest friends, who knew her conservative nature well, would be utterly astonished if they saw her in this state.

Naturally, she knew she would receive much attention and embraced it. She appeared different, reborn. Maybe this was exactly what she required after three weeks of an emotional and mental roller-coaster concerning her love life.

Initially, she experienced a slight sense of being left out, as Tiyan, Eki, and Ede were all now happily married. The situation worsened when, only two days ago, she received news of the birth of Prince Aimua, Eki's son. Ede announced she was pregnant, and Tiyan, who recently returned from her honeymoon, would probably announce any day now that she, too, was pregnant. Amenze had come to terms with the fact that she envied her friends and desired what they possessed.

The second reason for her emotional and mental roller-coaster was the prophecy. She believed that giving Dimitris her virginity would make marriage to the old king bearable. She returned to London ready to jump into bed with Dimitris before pulling the plug on the relationship.

But on the same day she returned to London, a fortnight before, she received a phone call which rattled her. The caller was Dimitris' older sister, Aphrodite. She asked Amenze to let Dimitris go. The request came as no surprise. Aphrodite made her dislike of Amenze very clear from the beginning, but it didn't bother Amenze, especially since she was uncertain about what the future had in store for her and Dimitris. It wasn't so much the phone call or the request to stay away from Dimitris that troubled Amenze; it was the fact that Aphrodite mentioned Dimitris' involvement with another woman. *Elena.* A woman their father handpicked for him to marry. A woman waiting on the side for his relationship with Amenze to end so they could become officially engaged.

Dimitris never mentioned such a woman. He never indicated that, for marriage, he already had a choice. Until that phone call, Amenze believed that Dimitris was seeing her alone. She wanted to call him after the call with Aphrodite, but she'd been too angry, and when she'd calmed down, he was out of London, and she decided to wait until he returned to speak to him in person. However, the couple of times she'd spoken to him on the phone since the chat with his sister, she had sensed his withdrawal from her.

She snapped out of her reverie to give attention to what Ero was saying and sensed the eyes boring into her back again. Despite being exposed, she experienced a warm sensation.

Ero winked at her mischievously. "Looks like you've caught Ogiame's eye."

Without meaning to, Amenze turned around and locked eyes with Bawo Domingo. In surprise, she let out a gasp. She had not thought to see him here, which was silly because this was a party for who's who within the African community in the United Kingdom. She was just surprised to run into him outside of the circle that Dimitris moved in.

She turned back to Ero. "That's Bawo Domingo of the House of Oma, right?"

She met him once, over a year ago, and it was pretty memorable. He was an alumnus of her university, having completed an MBA several years before. The school awarded him an honorary Doctor of Business Administration degree for his exemplary business prowess, and a large portrait of him hung in the student's lounge.

She spotted his portrait in the lounge in her second week of the MBA programme. His unusual attire caught and held her attention. He wore a well-tailored three-piece business suit along with boxing gloves. He stood like a boxer, too. She stood pondering its oddness when Dimitris Papadopoulos walked up to her.

"Bawo Domingo, my father's protégé," he informed her.

She turned to him, a little surprised he'd spoken to her because, until that point, they'd never spoken to each other in or outside of class.

"I am Dimitris," he introduced himself.

"Amenze," she supplied her name in response.

They spent the next few minutes discussing the portrait.

"What's with the business suit and the boxing gloves?" Amenze wanted to know. "The guy can't decide if he wants to be a business executive or a boxer?"

Dimitris shook his head. "I don't think that's it at all. If anyone knows what he wants, it's Bawo. Trust me. I wish I could answer your question, but I can't. But Bawo can. You can come with me next time I visit him."

That weekend, she accompanied Dimitris to an informal dinner party in Bawo's apartment in Mayfair. The Bawo she met significantly differed from the one in the portrait. Outside the picture, he was handsome, incredibly tall, and lean. His good looks had captivated Amenze. But that was not all. Bawo worked hard and played harder.

Amenze encountered not the consummate business executive but the serial player, who was dangerous to a woman's heart. He could not take his eyes off her from the moment she'd walked into his home, and he openly and unashamedly flirted with her. In the media room, he cornered her and kissed her breathless—as no man had ever kissed her. He invited her to spend the night, promising her breakfast on his yacht on the Mediterranean and dinner in Monaco. He laughed in her face when she told him she wasn't that kind of girl.

"Of course you are. Why else would you be here?" he sneered.

Amenze almost slapped his smug face. But she stayed calm as she searched for Dimitris and asked him to take her home. But not before she'd spoken her mind.

"You ought to be ashamed of yourself, Mr Domingo," she said. "I came here tonight because I respected and admired you. But you've completely ruined it."

As she progressed on her MBA journey, she learnt more about Bawo Domingo as she researched his business, the House of Oma, and its unique business model.

Her research of his business prompted her to research Bawo Domingo, the man. She'd come across gossip about him that made her wonder whether he had a PR team and whether they were doing their job at all. Every woman and her twin were on celebrity gossip websites and magazines, hinting at their intimate encounters with him.

She shook her head slightly as she forced herself away from her little daydream and into the present, where Ero answered her question.

"Yes, that's Bawo Domingo," he affirmed.

Amenze nodded as her brows came together. "Why did you call him Ogiame? You know that's a title reserved for the Olu of Warri, right?"

Ero shrugged. "It might be, but that's Domingo's moniker in our club."

Amenze turned again to look at the man across the room. He was no longer with Efua; he was an unfamiliar man. Both men looked about the same age and affluent in their bespoke tuxedos and designer shoes, but Bawo was taller and had a skin tone significantly lighter than his companion's very dark skin tone. He looked devilishly handsome, and his tuxedo moulded to the contour of his body, revealing a lean frame, broad shoulders, and a wide chest.

Amenze's mouth went dry as she gave him an appreciating glance, her eyes taking in every detail of his skin-fade hairstyle, which had lowly cut wavy hair near the top of the head that got shorter as it travelled down to the skin of his neckline. He smiled and slowly lifted his glass in salute. She glanced away and swallowed the rest of her champagne.

Ero, watching with keen interest, chuckled. "He's headed this way."

"So, I must be on my way," Amenze stated. "It was great talking to you, Ero. I am grateful that you allowed me to share a little about Elevate." As she turned away from Ero, she handed her stem glass to a passing waiter and moved quickly and elegantly in her four-inch stiletto heels. She kept walking until she reached the rooftop garden and sighed in relief.

*****

Where was the rest of her dress?

Bawo had asked that question as he initially entered the large ballroom of the stately home where the charity ball was held and set eyes on what had to be the softest, smoothest, well-toned back he had ever seen. As a former massage therapist, he had seen plenty of uncovered backs.

He'd been unable to approach her with all the people Suf wanted him to meet. After the banquet, he'd caught sight of the lean exposed back again and would have approached her then but got sidetracked by another woman who seemed bent on keeping him by her side, further annoying him.

He hadn't liked coming out tonight to support Kojo Boateng's charity. Kojo Boateng, a prominent rugby player with a Ghanaian father and English mother, was quite a sensation and the first black man to captain England's team before retiring a year ago. His early retirement from the game he loved, and which had brought him fame, was caused by a recent open-heart surgery to correct a heart defect he had been born with, but which did not manifest until he was in his early thirties and caused him to collapse in the middle of a game.

The world watched him go through diagnosis and treatment. He returned to play for a few months before announcing his retirement and mission to set up a charity to help children born with heart defects in Africa. The charity had successfully launched in Ghana months ago, and the first group of children, approximately ten of them, underwent successful heart surgeries. The UK launch event had a strong turnout, with rugby players past and present, celebrities from other sports, actors, actresses, and TV personalities in attendance.

Bawo had met Kojo several times as he and Suf were first cousins and great friends. Bawo liked Kojo but never cultivated a friendship with him. The man was married and too self-righteous for Bawo. His lousy influence got Suf into this prison, which he called a marriage. No doubt he had convinced Suf to take the plunge. It irritated Bawo when he thought about his friend rushing to get married. Zuhrah was a lovely woman, but he resented her for drastically changing his right-hand man and, by extension, the dynamics of their relationship.

"My name is Efua," his companion said. "Efua Boateng."

As she must have expected, the last name got him to turn and offer her one sweeping glance. She was no sister of Suf's. He knew Suf had no sister, only brothers. She was not mixed-race, so she could not be Kojo's…

"I'm Kojo Boateng's half-sister," she filled in the blank. "We have the same father but different mothers."

"That, I can see," he muttered dryly. He wanted to tell her to sod off but did not think Suf or Kojo would appreciate that. But he wished she would get lost, nonetheless. He wasn't here to look for a woman; if he wanted one, he'd found one the moment he walked in.

"You're the CEO of House of Oma. Suf works for you. I have been wanting to meet you."

"Have you now?" He stifled a groan. She had appeared at his side when Suf and Zuhrah disappeared to meet and greet members of the Boateng family who'd flown in from Africa to support their illustrious son. Surely, she wasn't here to babysit him? He could enquire if she knew the owner of that delectable backside. If she did, she could make herself useful and introduce him. The lady was now chatting with Ero Amadasun. He scowled.

"Efua?" he began, then paused. "That is your name, isn't it?"

The young woman nodded her head vigorously. "Yes, you're right. That is my name."

"Good," Bawo replied with a tight smile. "Would you tell me who the woman missing the back of her dress is?"

Efua snuck her arm through his and leaned closer so that her large breasts were brushing against his arm. That instant, the woman turned around, and Bawo sucked in his breath.

It was her! Dimitris' girlfriend! He would never forget that face. But she was different, much more elegant than he remembered. He made to move towards her, but she was turning away again and giving her attention to that wretched Ero Amadasun.

"You don't want to do that. She has a boyfriend."

Like I don't know!

"And where is he tonight?"

Efua shrugged. "I think he's out of town on business."

Bawo turned to gaze at his companion and winked mischievously. "That's convenient."

"What's convenient?"

Suf walked up to them, giving Bawo an apologetic smile over Efua's head, suggesting he had nothing to do with her clinging like a vine to his arm. Efua turned to him.

"Bawo has been ogling my flatmate over there. I've told him she's got a boyfriend, but…"

"Efua, why don't you go help me fetch Zuhrah?" Suf cut in.

Efua pouted, but she released Bawo's arm and walked away.

Bawo heaved a sigh of relief. "Thank you."

"Anytime, buddy!" Suf slapped him on the back. "Besides, I don't want you messing with my little cousin. Or any woman here, for that matter. I didn't bring you here to add to your current scandal. You're here to meet business prospects. And donate generously to the cause."

"Of course," Bawo responded dryly. "I'll meet any more prospects you want me to meet. And write Kojo a fat check. But first, I need to ask her to dance." He nodded towards Amenze across the room.

She turned to stare at him again as if on cue, and he raised his glass in salute. She looked away quickly. His smile broadened.

"Isn't that the same lady with the boyfriend?"

Bawo shrugged. "So?" Suf didn't know the half of it.

"So, imagine how that will help our deal with Chez Aboh if some guy starts complaining that you have stolen his woman."

Bawo scoffed, "She's hardly his woman if he lets her show up like that in public in his absence."

Suf pinched the bridge of his nose. "I don't like this, Bawo. Why didn't you bring a date with you?"

"I didn't feel like it. I've been bored lately."

It was true. He'd been in a state of restlessness and boredom. His life revolved around the same kind of women, the same circle, and the same social events, and he was getting tired. He craved something different. Perhaps a different type of woman. Like the one across the room. She was different. He'd realised it a little too late.

"But now you're not."

"Nope!" Bawo responded with enthusiasm, snapping out of his reverie. "Look at that skin, Suf. That back is calling for my hands to…"

"Enough!" Suf snapped. "You're going to do what you like, anyway. You always do. But please remember the deal with Aboh and how it hangs by a thread!"

"Of course," Bawo smirked. "And you have it all in control. Do you not?" He didn't wait for Suf to respond but slapped him on the back with a wicked glint in his eye.

A smile formed around his lips as he moved away from the slightly bewildered Suf and began to walk through the crowds of guests toward the object of his desire.

Was she trying to flee from him? He frowned. Was he losing his touch, or were his good looks fading, perhaps because of age? He touched his face. God forbid. She probably didn't want to talk to him after their first encounter. Regardless, he made a mental note to book a grooming session at one of his spas over the weekend.

CHAPTER FOUR

"Why did you run?" a voice behind her asked.

She whirled round to face its owner, already aware of his identity, before coming face-to-face with him. Did he pursue her up here? Or did he come here with a different purpose? She knew about his reputation with women, but tonight's party had an even larger number of beautiful women—from actresses to models to reality TV stars. They were more of his type. Why would he bother with her?

She came up here to distance herself from him, and for a moment, the beauty of her surroundings captivated her. The rectangular, sunken, torch-lit rooftop garden was vast and somewhat picturesque, with its well-kept, exotic, lush flowers. The air was delightful and fragrant.

"Mr…" she began, a little breathless. Did it result from walking and climbing the stairs, or was his presence constricting her breath?

"It's Bawo Domingo, but please call me Bawo."

He came closer, causing her to take a step backwards. "And what was your name again?"

"Amenze," she said. "Amenze Giwa-Amu."

"Ah, yes, Amenze. A beautiful name for a beautiful woman." Again, he took another step forward, eyeing her like a predator would eye a prey. Amenze took another step backwards.

"Why did you run from me?" he asked, with a slight frown as though the great Bawo Domingo could not imagine a woman trying to escape his clutches.

"I did not run from you."

What was this? Amenze wondered. *Were they going to carry on as if they hadn't met before? Would the elephant in the room be addressed at any time?*

"Yes, you did." He nodded as though to convince himself of his correctness. "I noticed you downstairs in the ballroom, and I was coming over to ask you to dance with me since your companion, Amadasun, didn't seem to know how to handle a beautiful woman. But as I approached, you fled. Literally." He took another step forward. Amenze stepped backwards until her back touched the solid concrete wall. He looked smug.

"I did not run." Her voice was nothing more than a whisper. Her heart increased its pace.

"You did." He put his hands on either side of the wall. "You appear frightened. Whatever you might think of me,

Amenze, I am a gentleman and never force a woman to do anything she's unwilling to do."

"I don't know you well enough to decide if that is true," she countered.

He smiled. "We must remedy that, beautiful Amenze." He put out a hand and gently touched her thick, glossy hair, enjoying its luxuriously soft texture between his finger and thumb, and then letting it go, but not before his fingers grazed her shoulder ever so slightly and sent tremors through her body. "Your hair's lovely. I like it this way. It looks better than the natural afro style you wore the last time. But I don't approve of the heavy makeup or the dress. While your skin is lovely, if you were my woman, I wouldn't want you showing off everything to all and sundry."

Amenze swallowed. Was he flirting with her? *Again*? "I am not your woman. I have a boyfriend. Dimitris."

"So, I've heard. But I don't see him here." He looked around him as if to stress the point. When he looked back at her, his eyes bore into hers. "Dance with me; Dimitris won't begrudge you that."

Like one in a daze, Amenze took his hand and let him lead her to the centre of the rooftop garden, where they stood under the rose arches. They could hear the music emitting from the ballroom. She went willingly as he pulled her into his arms, resting her head on his shoulder.

"Cold?" he murmured in her ear. He felt her slight shiver as his broad palm touched the slightly exposed small of her back.

She could not prevent him from stripping off his tuxedo jacket and wrapping it around her. His arms came around her again as they swayed in unison to the music.

"Better?" he whispered.

He put his hands on her back and pulled her closer, causing Amenze to stiffen and forget to breathe. She did not realise she was holding her breath until she heard him whisper in her ear in a sexy baritone.

"Breathe, Amenze. It's just a dance. I will do nothing untoward."

"Yes." She relaxed and shut her eyes, desiring this moment to last …forever…

But it didn't. The music stopped, and Amenze sighed almost wistfully as she stepped back.

"I think I should sit down now before I fall." She moved away to sit on an ornamental-looking garden bench.

"I would ask for another dance, even if it's to the music playing in my head, but you appear exhausted." He sat opposite her with long legs stretched out before him.

Amenze tried not to stare. "I am exhausted, and my feet hurt." She turned her attention to her feet.

Bawo's gaze instantly shifted to her feet. "Not surprising. Those must be very uncomfortable. Fashionable but uncomfortable and not sensible." He nodded toward her four-inch stilettoes.

"They are. Very uncomfortable," Amenze agreed, lifting a leg slightly.

Before she could stop him, Bawo leaned forward and bent over to undo her shoes. Amenze gasped. "What are you doing?"

"I'm going to give you a foot massage. Your blood circulation seems to be cut off by the straps."

Horrified, Amenze looked around the garden. There was nobody else around, and they were somewhat hidden beneath the arches. "But we're at a party," she protested.

"The party, what's left of it, is downstairs in the ballroom, Amenze. Up here, I think we're allowed to be undignified."

Amenze giggled and didn't stop him as he gingerly removed her shoes and placed her feet in his lap. She leaned back and shut her eyes as he massaged one foot and the other.

"That feels so good."

"I'm glad I haven't lost my touch after so many years."

Amenze opened her eyes to study his expressionless face. "Why did you stop being a massage therapist?"

Bawo shrugged. "I needed to expand my business and realised I wouldn't have the time to do so if I were occupied with giving massages." He paused thoughtfully and raised his head to study her. "But you already have information about my business, so you should know this. It's no secret."

Amenze wrapped his jacket around her more securely, enjoying its warmth and delighting in catching a whiff of his cologne. "True. I studied your business model and business while doing my MBA."

He lowered his head and gave attention to her feet. "I never imagined you as an MBA-holding woman."

"And I am currently pursuing a DBA."

"Beauty and brains." Bawo lifted his head and studied her. "I am impressed. The way your flatmate carried on about your boyfriend, anyone would have taken you for a kept woman."

"What?!" Amenze gasped. "That's the most ridiculous thing I ever heard. My parents raised me to work for my money. My father is a consultant gynaecologist, and so are my three older brothers. I come from a family that prides itself on hard work. I am no kept woman."

He studied her briefly, then lowered his gaze to her feet. "What do you do for a living besides studying towards a professional business doctoral degree?"

"Well, I run a business my friends and I set up."

"Impressive. Tell me more."

Amenze pulled her right foot back and stiffed a giggle. "Sorry. That was ticklish," she explained as Bawo seemed slightly bewildered by her reaction.

"You must be sensitive to tickling because I wasn't trying to tickle you." He grinned, making her doubt the sincerity of his words.

As she narrowed her eyes in a mock rage, he laughed, and she joined him.

"The business is called Elevate," she said as the laughter subsided. "The vision is to match Benin entrepreneurs with Benin investors."

"Remarkable," Bawo nodded, using alternating thumb movements up her right foot. "How long have you been around for?"

"About six months. Around two months ago, we hosted our first pitch event in Benin. But we have an office in London serving entrepreneurs and investors in the diaspora. We're currently planning a pitch event in London for next month."

He frowned as he gave his attention to massaging her toes. "How did I not know about this?"

Amenze stifled a yawn and shook her head slightly to ward off sleep. The foot massage was a lot more relaxing than she'd expected. "Possibly because you're neither a Benin entrepreneur nor a Benin investor. Besides, we're still new."

"I suppose that's why you talked to Ero Amadasun earlier?"

"Yes. I came out tonight mainly to network. These days, I am solely responsible for running Elevate as life with my closest friends is changing." Amenze sighed.

Bawo looked at her. "In what way?"

"My word! You ask a lot of questions!"

"A few people might agree, yes."

Amenze rolled her eyes. "Well, my friends became romantically involved and are now married. One has just become a mother, and the other has recently returned from her honeymoon."

"And you hope for the same thing? Marriage?" Bawo studied her briefly as his hands gently stretched out the arch of her foot.

Amenze sighed and pulled his jacket around her more closely. "Not marriage. I mean, not *just* marriage. Marrying the right man is a requirement. It seems silly because I always kept my head while my friends lost theirs to romantic foolishness, but once they met the men of their dreams, I yearned for the same experience, if that makes any sense."

"And you don't have that experience with Dimitris?"

"I prefer not to answer that," Amenze responded swiftly. "Do you miss giving massages?"

"No," he replied without looking at her. "It's how I started, but I would never have become rich that way. I had to train others and pass on my vision, and I am confident that they're giving the clients the best quality service possible, which is enough for me. So no, I don't miss being a massage therapist."

"Ero referred to you as Ogiame."

"Ero Amadasun and I belong to the same gentlemen's club, and it's a moniker I use in the club." He shrugged.

"That's probably because you're Itsekiri. Ogiame is a title reserved for the Itsekiri king."

"Yes, I am Itsekiri. I am surprised, you guessed. The Itsekiri people are not well-known among Africans.

"I am Benin, and the Benin kingdom shares a border with the Warri kingdom. Besides, my mother is Itsekiri, which makes me half-Itsekiri."

Bawo smiled up at her. "A woman after my heart. Do you speak the language?"

"Of course. What do you think? Itsekiri women are notorious for making their children Itsekiri regardless of where the child's father comes from."

Bawo nodded. "This is true."

"I think your name is beautiful. *Onetoritsebawoete*," she muttered and frowned as he jerked his head up in surprise.

"*Onetoritsebawoete*," she repeated. "It's your name. Isn't it? It means the one God backs does not fail."

"Yes. It's my name, and you know its meaning," he confirmed. "I'm astounded that you know it because it's not a very common Itsekiri name."

She shrugged. "Oh, my mum has a distant cousin who answers to the same name. She's called Ete for short."

He fell silent and gazed into her eyes. "Do you want to meet for dinner sometime and try some Itsekiri food?"

"That sounds divine." Amenze closed her eyes again and forgot where she was—everything except the sensation of Bawo's hands massaging her feet and the pleasure it aroused. But, like the dance, it would soon end.

"Amenze!"

Efua's voice caused Amenze to lift her feet off Bawo's lap. She turned toward the garden entrance and stared guiltily at her flatmate.

"There you are!" Efua looked from Bawo to Amenze. "We need to leave now. Kojo has a car and driver waiting to take us home." She turned to Bawo with a sweet smile. "It was lovely to meet you. I hope to see you again soon."

"Not if I can help it," Amenze heard Bawo mutter under his breath. She turned her gaze towards him, just as Efua did.

"Sorry?" Efua sounded confused.

"Have a good night, Efua."

Efua looked at him with a slight frown and turned to Amenze. "I'll be downstairs."

As Efua left, Amenze put her stiletto sandals on and rose to her feet. She took off Bawo's jacket and stretched it towards him as he stood to his feet. "Thank you. My shawl's downstairs in the cloakroom. I'll grab it on my way out."

"I'm coming with you." He wrapped the jacket around her and walked with her down the stairs. He never let her out of his sight until she got into the car. And just before she did, he handed her his business card. "Text me when you get home, and we'll plan that dinner."

Bawo watched the car carrying Amenze until it disappeared from sight. Their meeting didn't quite go as he envisioned, but it wasn't a disaster, unlike the previous instance. He'd wanted to apologise for his behaviour the last time, but somehow, they'd skirted the issue without bringing it up.

He'd intended to become acquainted with her without flirting. But he'd flirted like the first time. The woman made him act on impulse. He needed to regain control and exude a cool attitude henceforth. He wanted to be a friend and bide his time. Dimitris would break up with her soon, and he hoped to provide comfort as a friend and establish a romantic relationship as her boyfriend. He recoiled.

Boyfriend? What boyfriend? He must be losing the plot!

He wasn't anybody's boyfriend. Long-term relationships were not his thing. He had affairs, no-strings-attached arrangements, where both parties knew the score, and then he moved on. However, it didn't feel suitable for Amenze. He remembered how she'd rebuked him that first night, and he smiled despite himself. No woman had spoken to him like that. Yes. She was different. *Special.*

As he slipped his jacket back on, he relished he had wrapped it around her only moments ago. He turned to return to the building, but Suf stood before him, blocking his way.

He groaned, "What now?"

"Bawo, if you told me you would marry that young lady, I'd be willing to forgive you for all the trouble that's likely to come to our door when Efua rattles off to her boyfriend what you've been up to tonight."

He sighed, thrusting his hands deep into his pockets. Not this talk of marriage again. "Remind me again why I can't fire you."

"You can. Except it will cost you a lot in legal fees, plus also cost you a good friend and brother-in-arms," Suf said. "I need say no more."

He returned to the ballroom. Bawo would have followed, but his phone vibrating caused him to stand still. He pulled the phone out of his pocket and answered the call.

"Who is this?"

"Prince Ajoritsedere Toritseju Esijolomisan Tunoka," the caller responded.

"Sod off!" Bawo stated through gritted teeth and cut the call.

CHAPTER FIVE

"Woah! Take a deep breath, Imatiti!"

Amenze rose from her swivel chair and paced the large, impressively furnished open-plan office she shared with her team members. Its ceiling-to-floor windows brought in plenty of natural light and the commuters' hustle and bustle of activities around London Bridge.

Amenze stood by the window, trying to appreciate the view of the Thames, the red buses, black cabs, tourists, and the little things that made London unique. Perhaps she needed to calm down more than the woman on the phone. With one hand slid into the pocket of the cream-tailored pants she'd styled nicely with a coffee-coloured silk blouse and nude Michael Kors pumps, Amenze shut her eyes and counted to ten.

"Relax, Imatiti, there is absolutely no need to panic. We're here to hold your hand every step of the way." Amenze allowed time for her words and their meaning to sink in.

Imatiti, a Benin small business entrepreneur who recently subscribed to Elevate's services, was scheduled to pitch her new business to investors at the upcoming Elevate pitch event. She was a brilliant entrepreneur with an exceptional business plan and a thriving startup, but she lacked confidence, which begged the question of how she'd made her business successful.

The woman possessed zero faith in herself and her ability to pitch her business idea successfully to a handful of investors. She worried about everything going wrong and about rejection.

Amenze listened patiently as Imatiti rambled off at the end of the line, saying many things yet saying nothing. After a few minutes, Amenze politely cut her off before she killed what little shred of confidence *she* enjoyed.

"Imatiti, listen to me. I realise you haven't done this before, and you are scared. But I assure you, it will be okay. You have one full month to practise and perfect your pitch," Amenze assured her, not for the first time.

"Will you tell me again what to expect?" Imatiti begged. "I appreciate that you have mentioned it before, but I don't think I properly understood it."

"Okay. On that day, you will stand before the investors and pitch your wonderful business idea to them like you've pitched it to me almost daily for the last fortnight." Amenze paused to allow the information to sink in.

"When you're done, the investors will have some questions for you. They will ask about your business model, your unique selling point, target customers, what traction you have so far, how you will make revenue, how quickly your business could become profitable, who your core team members are and their experience, what your long-term vision is and the growth potential of your business. These are some questions to anticipate."

"Thank you," Imatiti mumbled. "The information is helpful, but it's overwhelming right now.

"Yes. It is, and we're not expecting you to take it all in right now. It's all in the email that's being sent to you today. Go over it and call me if you have questions."

Amenze paused and listened with an empathetic ear to Imatiti, remembering to keep a smile on her face. Long ago, she learned that people may not see your smile, but they heard it or the lack of it in your voice.

"Thank you for your help, Amenze. I am so sorry I came close to having a meltdown just now.

"That's fine, Imatiti. We are here to help you. Have a wonderful day. Bye."

Amenze ended the call and moved away from the window, tossing the mobile phone on the meticulously tidy desk and dropping into the high-backed chair with an exaggerated sigh. When this pitch event for Benin investors and entrepreneurs in the diaspora ended, she would go on an extended vacation.

She gazed up at Joan, whose desk faced hers. Joan served as her assistant and the office manager. As if on cue, Joan looked up from her desktop screen.

"Is Imatiti okay?"

"She is for now. Hopefully, she will be on D-day." Amenze shook her head. "Joan, please send the pitch preparation email to all the entrepreneurs on our mailing list, regardless of whether they're pitching in this coming event."

"I will get it done right away."

"Also, can you reschedule my afternoon appointments? I am meeting Ero Amadasun for lunch, so I will be out of the office. Fingers crossed; today is the day we sign him on as an investor."

Joan gave her a thumbs up. "Make it happen, Amenze," she urged.

"I will," Amenze assured her. "He seemed quite interested when I talked to him at the charity ball last night. That he wants to see me today is a positive sign he wants to go forward."

"Yes. I think so, too. Good luck."

"Thank you, Joan. See if you can arrange a conference call for me with Eki and Tiyan sometime this week or next week. The earlier, the better. I appreciate they have a lot going on in their lives now, but I need clarification about the pitch event, so schedule some time in the diaries."

"I am on it." Joan picked a pen and scribbled the instructions on a little notepad.

Amenze started to make another request when the receptionist walked in with an enormous bouquet of yellow roses.

"What is this?" Amenze exclaimed.

"I should ask you that," Paula, the bubbly receptionist, stated as she put the bouquet on Amenze's desk. "They are for you."

"Oh, my!" Joan excitedly rose from her desk and walked to Amenze's desk to inspect the bouquet closely. "That boyfriend of yours has outdone himself this time."

Amenze frowned. How did she inform these women that she was yet to get flowers from Dimitris? She said nothing as she rose from her chair and pulled out the card. Both women watched her with great interest. Glowering at them, she walked towards the windows and read the note.

Amenze,

This is eighteen months too late, but I hope you will forgive me for my rudeness and allow me to regain your respect and admiration.

Bawo.

Amenze smiled. She found the apology to be the sweetest one she had ever received. How could she remain upset, assuming that she was still angry? Not after last night. Not after the thoughtful side of himself, he'd revealed last night. And certainly not after this grand gesture. This was a delightful surprise as she hadn't anticipated it.

"Well, what does it say?" Paula asked.

"Are you still there?" Amenze spun on her heels and glowered at both women a second time. It didn't work. She rolled her eyes. "Okay. It's from a friend. He is making amends for a wrong he did."

"Well, that's big enough to right any wrong." Joan nodded towards the bouquet.

"Yes. It's so sweet," Paula added.

Amenze rolled her eyes and returned to her seat, putting the card away in her drawer.

"I'll put these in water for you." Joan took the flowers away. Thankfully, Paula returned to her desk in the outer office and asked no more questions.

Amenze picked up her mobile phone and texted Bawo.

The flowers are beautiful. Thank you.

She set aside her phone and attempted to focus on the report she was writing to inform the Elevate members about the progress made thus far concerning the upcoming pitch event. Her mind wandered, unable to focus on the task at hand. She eagerly expected his response and wondered how long it would take. It took three minutes, and her phone beeped. She looked away from her laptop and reached for the phone.

Joan returned with the enormous bouquet immersed in a crystal vase filled with water and gingerly placed it on the edge of Amenze's desk.

"Thank you, Joan." Amenze looked up at Joan, who stood admiring the flowers.

"They're beautiful." Joan sniffed them appreciatingly before turning to her desk.

Amenze looked down at the phone in her hand and read Bawo's message.

They're not as beautiful as you, but I am glad you like them. Does this mean my apology is accepted?

Amenze's smile widened. While in the process of replying, she glanced up and discovered Joan observing her.

"What?"

Joan shrugged. "Nothing." She peered at her desktop screen. "You seem happy."

"I am always happy." Amenze rolled her eyes and looked back at her phone.

Tell me one thing first. Did you choose them yourself?

She sent the message but did not put down the phone as she waited excitedly for his response. It came quickly. She opened it and read.

Yes, I did. It never occurred to me to ask anyone else to.

He knew the right words to say to a woman. Amenze laughed softly as she quickly texted back.

Yes. Your apology is accepted.

She put the phone away and returned to her report—but not for long. Soon, her phone vibrated, and she almost immediately picked it up. Leaning back in her chair, she opened the message and read.

That is an immense relief. I can sleep better tonight. Sorry, it's coming late. Last night, I wanted to apologise but was uncertain how to proceed.

Better late than never. She texted in response and put the phone aside with a smile. Within seconds, it beeped again, and she laughed softly and picked it up. She glanced at Joan, but the other woman was engrossed in the task before her and no longer watching Amenze. Amenze heaved a small sigh of relief as she read Bawo's text.

Have you eaten lunch? I can pick you up and take you some place nice.

Amenze read the message and felt a slight twinge of disappointment. She would have said yes, but she had a business lunch with Ero. With a wistful sigh, she texted back.

I haven't eaten lunch. But I am going to turn down your offer. I am meeting Ero Amadasun for a late lunch.

His reply came quickly before she put down the phone.

Is it business?

Amenze sighed. *God, give me patience,* she thought in mock exasperation.

Yes. It's business. Not that it's any of your business.

She chuckled softly as she hit the send button on her phone.

*****

Bawo grinned as he read her message and realised he'd been rebuked. He quickly typed a response.

I'm glad it's business. We'll have lunch some other time.

He read the message and hit the send button. His words did not reflect the truth. Business or not, he didn't want

Amenze meeting Ero Amadasun or any other man for lunch. Not that he would tell her that. She would doubtless scold him if he dared. He chuckled as he recalled their first meeting and how she'd reprimanded him. She possessed spunk; he'd give her that.

"Are you with me?"

At Suf's question, Bawo slowly lifted his head from his mobile device. Suf stood a few feet from Bawo's imposing desk, his iPad held in one hand, and the other hand inserted into the pants of his dark pinstriped business suit. His expression, while looking at Bawo, conveyed disapproval and anticipation of a response. A response to what, exactly? Bawo racked his brain.

"You're not with me," Suf concluded. "It can't be what I said that's caused you to laugh. Did you hear a word I said in the last five minutes?"

Bawo frowned as he tried to recall the last five minutes. He found himself unable to recall the details of the conversation with Suf. He realised Suf had been speaking to him, but he did not remember his words.

"I was right. You were distracted." Suf scratched his head in exasperation. "I hope that's not who I think it is." He nodded towards the phone.

"And who might that be?" Bawo put the phone aside and moved his attention to his laptop. A spreadsheet was open before him, and until he received Amenze's text, he had been happily examining and analysing numbers. Now, his interest in it had dissipated entirely. With a mouse flick, he moved the spreadsheet from his laptop screen to the bigger monitor, which sat on his desk behind the laptop.

Suf placed his iPad at the edge of the desk and put his hands on the desk, allowing him to lean closer to Bawo. "The young woman from last night. Efua's flatmate."

Bawo kept his eyes fixed on the screen, pretending to be deeply engrossed in the numbers on the spreadsheet even though he saw nothing. "I don't need a lecture, Suf. I am aware she has a boyfriend, and I am not doing anything amorous. She is Itsekiri, or at least her mother is, and we're simply bonding over that."

"Listen to yourself, Bawo," Suf sneered. "You are bonding over that. You have Emami here. She's been working for you for over five years. She's Itsekiri but you've yet to bond with her over that."

The thought of trying to bond with Emami over anything had Bawo in stitches. He threw back his head and roared with laughter, and Suf joined him.

Emami Diden was a small, stern-looking Itsekiri woman in her early fifties. She lived a life of solitude, having never married, and served as Bawo's private secretary, overseeing the operations of his offices and residences with exceptional efficiency and discretion. She was Bawo's trusted assistant, and he was lost without her. It helped, too, that she was Itsekiri, making it possible for Bawo to give her instructions in the language for utmost discretion, but he would not bond with her over that or anything else ever.

Emami entered the office. She looked severe in her dark grey, well-tailored pantsuit and her braided hair was pulled back from her face. She pushed her spectacles up the bridge of her nose and peered at Suf through the upper part of her bifocals. Her expression was a silent reprove she reserved for him whenever he stayed too long in Bawo's office. While the two worked well together, Emami, the ever-efficient gatekeeper, allowed no one, not even Suf, to waste Bawo's precious time. Suf straightened almost immediately and picked up his iPad in preparation to leave.

Emami turned to Bawo and attempted a smile as she locked eyes with him. "Your one-o'clock appointment is here, Bawo," she announced. "Shall I ask him to come in?"

"Give me five minutes to finish with Suf, and then send him in," Bawo advised. Suf was still in his office because he hadn't been paying attention. But Emami didn't know this; she gave Suf another disapproving stare before turning to Bawo.

"Can we catch up after your appointment? I need to review your calendar for the rest of the week and reconcile some arising clashes."

Bawo grimaced. The conflicts solely stemmed from his actions. He constantly made appointments and said yes to engagements without checking his calendar. Poor Emami continually resolved appointment clashes.

He flashed her an apologetic grin. "Yes, we can do that after my appointment while I'm having lunch," he confirmed, and Emami left. Since Amenze wasn't available for lunch, he'd have his usual green club sandwich at his desk while he worked.

"What was it you wanted, Suf? I am sorry I got distracted." Bawo gave Suf his undivided attention as soon as the door shut behind Emami.

"Do you need me in Paris for the House of Oma Tower opening?"

Bawo frowned as he contemplated the question for a moment. He shook his head. "I don't think I need you there. Besides, it's the same weekend you're off to that property developers' meeting in Dubai, isn't it?"

Suf nodded. "Yes, but I can reschedule or send someone in my place if you need me in Paris, which is why I am asking."

Bawo shook his head. "No. You go on to Dubai. I can manage Paris alone. I might take Emami with me."

"That should be a wonderful bonding experience," Suf jeered as he walked towards the door.

"Go to hell, Suf!"

CHAPTER SIX

"Ooh…"

Amenze groaned and covered her head with a pillow. No. That would never do. The noise persisted. She groaned again as she threw aside the pillow and rolled over in bed just enough to reach out a hand and hit the snooze button on her annoying alarm.

That should shut it up for another ten minutes, she thought smugly as she lay back on the pillows and shut her eyes, relishing the quietness of the morning. She had placed her alarm on snooze for ten minutes; now, if she could equally sleep for ten minutes, she'd be okay—or so she thought. She was completely drained of energy as she barely got any sleep last night.

She accepted that she should not have stayed up late holding the conference call with Eki and Tiyan. It had been a bad idea, but she missed her friends, and it had been great to catch up with them to discuss Elevate and the current happenings in their lives. Eki had been eager to show off her gorgeous baby boy, Prince Aimua. It was late, and the tot was fast asleep in his crib, but that had not stopped Eki from taking the mobile device into his nursery so Amenze and Tiyan could see the tiny, swaddled baby as he slept.

It was so surreal. Eki wasn't only a wife but a mother, and what a peaceful, gorgeous baby she had. He did not stir as his mother fussed over his sleeping form, talking endlessly about how he hardly ever cried and all he did was eat and sleep. He was so beautiful. Amenze couldn't wait to see him and give him a big cuddle.

They rejoiced over his arrival and celebrated Tiyan's pregnancy news. Both friends urged her to hook Dimitris as they wanted to see her get married and have a baby soon.

"Our kids will be in the same age bracket and grow up together. It'll be so much fun!" Eki enthused.

Amenze had remained quiet so as not to throw water and dampen the mood. Soon enough, they would discover that things wouldn't work between herself and Dimitris, and they'd find out about the prophecy.

They talked until past 1 am, and then she went to bed but didn't sleep immediately as she again compared her life with Eki and Tiyan's. She would've had ample time to catch up with her sleep any other day, but this morning, she had to be at the airport early to pick her mother up. Her mother was arriving today from Benin and would spend the night before leaving for America the following morning to visit Amenze's older brothers and their families. So Amenze had cleared her diary for today so she could be at her mother's beck and call. Not entirely, though. She was having dinner with Bawo tonight.

She smiled as she recalled the last two weeks since she'd met Bawo again at the charity ball. After surprising her the following day with an enormous bouquet of yellow roses, he dropped by her office the next morning, armed with coffee and croissants. She'd been pleasantly surprised, especially since he'd bought her white coffee. It turned out he had a very resourceful private secretary who'd made it her business to get the information from Paula.

He'd hung around, and they'd chatted over coffee and croissants. Then he'd left for his office. She did not see him for four days, but they'd texted each other almost non-stop during that entire time. Then, on day five, she'd returned from work, and nearly an hour later, he'd shown up at her front door unannounced.

"I came to feed you," he'd said with a grin when she'd opened the front door and expressed surprise at seeing him.

Amenze had let him in, especially as he'd arrived laden with takeout from her favourite Thai restaurant. They'd eaten and chatted about their workday, and he'd left. She'd not seen him since then as he'd travelled around Europe looking after his business concerns. But he'd texted her every night so much it had become a nighttime routine she looked forward to. She had missed him and looked forward to seeing him tonight.

Her alarm rang again, interrupting her reverie. She grumbled as she threw back the covers, got out of bed, and prepared to leave for the airport.

The day passed swiftly. Sisi Tuedor filled the time with many stories about the happenings in Benin since Amenze's last visit. Anyone would think Amenze hadn't been in Benin for years. But Amenze indulged her, even listening again to stories her mother had already shared with her over the phone.

She was relieved when, after a late breakfast, Sisi Tuedor retired to the bedroom to get some sleep. Amenze nipped out to get groceries and run errands for her mother. She returned to the flat in time to make her lunch.

At about 6 pm, Efua arrived home from work. She'd never met Amenze's mother, but Amenze had told Efua a little about her mother and told her mother a little about Efua. Efua had known Amenze's mother would be around for a night, so once she stepped in and saw the plump, middle-aged woman in an Ankara kaftan dress sprawled on the couch, she put on a broad smile so plastic, Amenze rolled her eyes.

"Good evening, ma'am." Although she sounded cheerful, Amenze detected her nervousness from the rigidity of her back.

"Hello, Efua," Amenze greeted as her mother delayed answering. Amenze held her breath. Her mother hated to be addressed as ma'am and told off a friend of her brother's years ago. Amenze hoped she didn't do the same to Efua.

"Good evening," came the curt reply. Efua immediately spun on her heels and fled to her room. Amenze thought she would probably stay in there until Sisi Tuedor left the following morning.

Amenze turned to her mother when Efua's bedroom door shut behind her. "Mum, that wasn't nice."

"I am not sure what you mean," Sisi Tuedor replied. "Did you tell her she can call me ma'am?"

"Of course not," Amenze answered. As if she would dare. This was her fault; she should have told Efua how to address her mother.

"Ma'am!" Sisi Tuedor snorted. "The cheek of it. Am I her mother?"

"No, Mum, you're not. And next time, I will tell my friends how to address you." Amenze's voice conveyed her annoyance as she stood and strolled off to her bedroom to prepare for her evening with Bawo. She wore a black one-shoulder jumpsuit that left a shoulder bare and moulded nicely to her upper body, emphasising curved and perky breasts. The bottom flared out in a charming, pleated palazzo style, and the decorative gold chain belt highlighted her delicate, slim waist. A four-inch pair of Jimmy Choo heels enhanced her height and nicely completed the outfit. Her hair, recently straightened, fell to one side over her bare shoulder. She applied her favourite perfume to her pulse points and sought out Efua to apologise for her mother's behaviour.

She found Efua in her room watching Netflix on her tablet and tucking into an Indian takeout she brought home from work. Amenze tried to apologise, but Efua waved it off, eyeing Amenze from head to toe and more interested in her outfit than in the apology.

"Big date tonight?" she wanted to know. "Is Dimitris back in London?"

"First, it's not a date, not really, and it is with Bawo Domingo."

Efua's eyes widened in shock. "What exactly is going on between you two? You have a boyfriend, and you are cheating on him right now, and Bawo is a playboy who is going to use you and dump you!"

Amenze held up her hands. "Efua, calm down. There is no need to get worked up. If I am cheating on Dimitris, that's between him and me, and you don't need to concern yourself with it. If Bawo is going to use me and dump me, it's between him and me and need not concern you."

Efua shrugged and swallowed her food. "Just watch your back."

"I intend to, Efua."

As Amenze walked into the living room, the doorbell rang. "That must be Bawo."

"That must be who?" Sisi Tuedor asked, taking her eyes off the television set and eyeing Amenze's change of clothes. "Are you going out?"

"Yes, I am, Mum. I will be back late, so don't wait for me. Your dinner is in the fridge; you can microwave it when you're ready."

"You don't need to worry about me. I can find my way around a kitchen. Now, please let the young man in." Sisi Tuedor gently sat up on the couch.

Amenze smiled as she opened the door to reveal Bawo—a casual-looking Bawo. He'd swapped the business suit for designer pants and a designer sweatshirt. He looked so handsome her smile faltered, as did her heart.

He's gorgeous, she thought. She'd forgotten how good-looking he was.

"Please come in."

As Bawo entered the room, Sisi Tuedor stood to her feet.

"Mum, this is my friend, Bawo, who, coincidentally, is Itsekiri. Bawo, this is my mother, my Itsekiri mother, Tuedor Giwa-Amu."

Instantly, Bawo smiled and bowed slightly, "Do, Sisi," he said, causing Sisi Tuedor's smile to widen. "Good evening, and welcome to London."

"*Edema we o sengua.*" Sisi Tuedor nodded her approval before turning to Amenze. "I like this young man, Amenze." Without waiting for Amenze's response, she turned back to Bawo. "*Edema boko?* How are you? Good evening to you. I am from the Ikomi family, but married to Amenze's father, a Benin man, for over three decades. And your family is?"

"Domingo, Sisi," he responded, bowing again slightly.

"Wonderful. I have heard of the Domingo family. It's quite a large one and famous for being the first Itsekiri people to interact with the Portuguese."

"This is correct, Sisi," Bawo answered.

"Well, I will leave you two alone. Enjoy your outing." Sisi Tuedor left the room.

Amenze turned to address Bawo. "Please have a seat; I need to grab my purse. I will only be a minute."

Amenze entered the room on her mother's heels. "I just need to grab my purse," she announced, as her mother looked surprised to see her.

"That's fine," Sisi Tuedor sat on the edge of the bed. "I like the young man, Amenze."

"Yes, Mummy, you already said that. In his presence."

Sisi Tuedor looked lost in her thoughts, her arms folded across her breasts, a smile on her lips. "He is an Itsekiri man of good breeding. He addressed me correctly, unlike that silly girl calling me ma'am. I think he will be a good choice for a husband. Play your cards right."

"Seriously, Mother? Bawo and I don't have that kind of relationship. I only recently made his acquaintance." True, if she didn't count her first meeting with Bawo. And she thought it was probably best she didn't mention that, or her mother may very well have come up with a prophecy to rival Usi's.

Sisi Tuedor looked irritated as she turned to Amenze. "Please stop being so naive. What do you mean you only just met him? I saw how the young man looked at you when he arrived. You are holding him back; may you be delivered from foolishness. If you give him the green light, you will not return from this date a virgin."

Amenze gasped. "Mummy! What a scandalous statement to make."

"I have spoken the truth. You better play your cards right. That's a handsome, rich, respectful man you have there and in the United Kingdom, where your father's cousins couldn't find a husband. If you mess up this opportunity, you have yourself to blame. That flatmate of yours who was wriggling her buttocks earlier will snatch him from under your nose. I know her kind. I won't be surprised if she's already trying to chat him up in the living room."

"So, you want me to sleep with Bawo?"

Sisi Tuedor looked annoyed. "Oh, stop this nonsense! I haven't asked you to sleep with anybody, but you are an Itsekiri woman, and you should know how to get a man and keep him. When I met your father years ago, he was engaged to a Benin woman. I was just the young lady who lived down the road and said hello when I passed him on the streets. Then, an accident left him wearing a cast and using crutches for six months.

"His so-called fiancée disappeared. I took it upon myself to see him daily, cook his meals, clean his house, and do his laundry. When his fiancée showed up, I was pregnant, and my bride price was about to be paid. If I said we didn't have that kind of relationship, where would it have got me? You must be intentional, seize opportunities, and take what you want, or another woman will."

"You seem to forget the prophecy."

Sisi Tuedor laughed mirthlessly. "Are we back to the prophecy? I thought you vehemently rejected the idea of marrying Olu Ginuwa III?"

"Yes, I did, and I do!" Amenze angrily picked up her purse and returned to the living room, where Bawo stood engrossed in a chat with Efua. They stopped as she entered the room and looked guilty, or perhaps she imagined it. Possibly because of her mother's earlier comments, she didn't like seeing Bawo with Efua.

Was she jealous? No, she couldn't be.

"I like your mother," Bawo informed her as they drove away in his black Jaguar SUV.

"She likes you too." Amenze glanced at him, and their eyes met and held for a fraction of a second before he looked back at the road. "Calling her Sisi made her fall in love with you. Efua called her ma'am only an hour before, and she'd been fuming."

Bawo chuckled. "If there's one thing I learnt early in life, it was to address an elderly Itsekiri woman as Sisi."

"Well, you learnt well." Amenze beamed at him before looking out the window to watch the remnants of the rush-hour traffic.

"I hope you're hungry?"

"Hungry enough to eat a horse."

Bawo nodded. "Good. That's what I like to hear after slaving over a hot stove."

Amenze laughed. "You're funny. You forget I attended one of your dinner parties. Bawo, I understand what your slaving over a hot stove involves. You have caterers on speed dial. They come in, set up in your kitchen, cook and serve the guests, and clean up. That's not my idea of slaving over a hot stove."

Bawo took his eyes off the road and looked at her with a glint of amusement. "Is that what you think I've done? Called in caterers?"

Amenze shrugged. "Sure, why not? It's what you did before."

"This is different. It is a quiet meal for two and traditional Itsekiri food. I doubt that the caterers I have on speed dial can make Itsekiri food."

"Bawo, you strike me as a very resourceful man. I'm sure you can find caterers in London to make Itsekiri food. Perhaps that's the difficulty you describe as slaving over a hot stove."

Bawo shook with laughter. "You are in for a surprise."

CHAPTER SEVEN

"Did you cook all this yourself?"

There was a look of disbelief on Amenze's face as she stood in the spacious, well-lighted dining room adjoining his open-plan kitchen, a glass of sparkling apple juice in one hand, watching him arrange food on the white oval table.

Bawo looked up from setting the dinner table. "Yes, I did."

"You can cook?"

He grinned ear to ear as he walked into the kitchen to retrieve the massive clay pot of catfish banga soup, which bubbled delightfully as he carried it to the table. He placed it gently in an equally large glass bowl half-filled with water.

He glanced up at her once he finished. "Pick your jaw off the floor."

Amenze laughed out loud as she realised her mouth had been hanging open. "I am shocked that you cook."

"You sound like you find that hard to believe." Bawo returned to the kitchen and removed his apron and oven gloves.

"That's because I do."

"Why?" He joined her again in the dining room and held a chair for her to sit down. "Can't you cook? Didn't your mother teach you to cook?"

"Of course she did. But I am a female, and in African culture, women must learn to cook and maintain the house. That's not expected of men, so the men who can cook are an exception to the rule."

"I see what you mean," Bawo replied as he pulled out a chair and sat beside her. "I took an interest in cooking from an early age, so my aunt, Sisi Alero, taught me."

Amenze frowned. "Not your mum?"

"My mum died giving birth to me."

Bawo mentally kicked himself. He did not mention his mother's death. Ever. What was it about this woman that made him act without thinking? He did not understand it and possibly needed time to process it all. And he hadn't had time, had he? They texted back and forth if he wasn't with her, sometimes while he was in business meetings. It was unprecedented. Even this dinner, cooking for her, showing her this other side of him, inviting her to his sacred space, where he never brought women or socialised; what was it all about?

Why did he have to show her a part of his life that he kept from others? Why tell her about his mother's death during his birth? What would he tell her next? Would he tell her about his father? Almost as soon as the thought crossed his mind, he vigorously rejected it.

No!

He dragged himself back to the moment as they ate the meal he had spent hours cooking. There was pepper soup cooked with goat meat and boiled yams and plantains; okra pepper soup made with grilled fish, periwinkles, and shrimp; *ukodo*, a traditional spicy yam pottage; and catfish banga soup and starch. He also prepared a large platter of spicy snails and prawns.

Amenze sampled everything with relish. He loved watching her eat, delighted in her enjoyment of the Itsekiri traditional meals. He was sick to the stomach of pretentious women who constantly picked at their food and bore him to tears with talk of calories, caloric deficit, and weight loss.

"I see you enjoy good food," he said. "The chef is suitably complimented."

"It's delicious. Everything tastes divine," Amenze replied. "My mother didn't only teach me to cook; she also taught me to appreciate good cooking. As a child, I remember watching her eat starch and banga soup. You could tell the soup was delicious by how she licked and smacked her lips."

Bawo nodded. "A true Itsekiri woman. She reminds me of my aunt. Is she around for a while?"

"On no. Thankfully, she leaves for America tomorrow morning to spend a week with her favourite children. My older brothers."

"You sound pleased."

"I am. I love my mother, but she's a typical Itsekiri woman, meaning she can be a handful."

Bawo frowned. "In what way?"

"I picked her up from the airport this morning, and we travelled in a cab going to my flat. The cab driver was chatty. You know how they can be sometimes. My mother hates it, and she's told me it only ever happens to her when she comes to London. So, as soon as the driver started chatting, my mother pinched me in the backseat and said, *Aghan da wa ren*, here they come again. The driver was oblivious and continued chatting away, and she put her hands on her head and said, *Mo ku ren*, I am dead!"

Bawo threw back his head and roared with laughter.

After dinner, Amenze helped him clear the table and load the dishes into the dishwasher. When they finished, he took her on a tour around the house. He loved his townhouse in Chelsea; a four-bedroom house spread over three floors, with a spacious, elaborately tiled courtyard in the centre bounded by glass walls on all four sides. The courtyard was adorned with a crystal-clear acrylic pool, rather than a skyline roof. It was stunning and cost him a small fortune.

As they entered his home office on the second-floor landing, Amenze surprised him by making a beeline for the pair of boxing gloves in a glass case sitting on his desk.

"I remember these," she announced excitedly. "There's a portrait of you at my university, and you're wearing a business suit and these gloves. Why?"

He grinned, delighted by her interest. Dimitris was correct when he introduced her as a star-struck fan that first night. She'd probably been bursting with questions, but he'd lusted after her and not given her a chance to talk to him.

"It's a long story, which I won't bore you with tonight. But the boxing gloves represent my courage and determination expressed in a willingness to fight for my vision." He reached out and stroked the glass case as he spoke. "The gloves symbolise how hard I fought to get where I am and must continue to fight. They also remind me of my motto: life is a battlefield, and nothing worthwhile is attained without a fight."

"That's the most remarkable thing I've ever heard."

"I'm glad you think so." His heart skipped a beat as she moved past him to the wall where his mother's portrait hung.

"Is this your mum?" She turned to look at him to verify the resemblance.

"Yes. That's Oma Domingo." He shoved his hands deep in his pockets as he prepared for what came next. Fortunately, she didn't ask questions.

"She's stunning. You look a lot like her."

"So, I'm handsome?"

Amenze pursed her lips. "You know you are; stop fishing for compliments."

Her look of disapproval reminded him of their first meeting. He laughed softly as he took her hand, and they continued their tour of the rest of the house, ending on the rooftop terrace with the swimming pool.

"It is so beautiful up here, Bawo," Amenze gushed as she took in the stunning rooftop view, the main seating area with its cream and coffee contemporary minimalist furniture, and the large skyline swimming pool with submersible colour-changing pool lights.

"Thank you," Bawo responded, pleased that she liked his home. "I think so too. It's one of my favourite parts of the house. Not that I get enough time to enjoy it."

"That's such a shame." Amenze lovingly ran a hand over the back of the plush two-seater sofa.

Now would be a good time to ask her to swim. He planned for them to swim, bought her a bikini, and looked forward to seeing her in it.

Go on then and ask her, the voice in his head urged, but he quelled it.

He would not ask her. If a bikini-clad Amenze got into his pool with him, his hands would be all over her. There'd be no swimming. She would think he planned the dinner date to seduce her.

But you did, the voice reminded him. Again, he silenced it.

Yes, he planned this dinner date, hoping to seduce Amenze, but right now, he sensed the timing was wrong. He would be reprimanded. It might be best to find another way to pass the rest of the evening—something that would allow him to touch her, but not so intimately that he'd be told off.

"You have a beautiful house," Amenze smiled at him. "Thank you for showing it to me."

"I took great pleasure in showing it to you." He took her hand and led her back downstairs to the living room, where he offered her some wine and a foot massage. Her eyes widened with excitement.

"You're going to give me another foot massage?"

"Yes, I am," he affirmed, leading her to the cream leather single armchair recliner. "Didn't you enjoy the last one?"

"I did."

"Good. That's what I like to hear. But be warned, if you've got smelly feet, I will renege on my promise and throw you out."

She took his joke good-naturedly and burst out laughing. He liked her laughter and easy-going personality.

Bawo filled a glass with wine, handed it to Amenze, and then removed her shoes. Her feet were slender and pretty, and he loved them. He looked up at her, and their eyes met and held. Memories of their first kiss in his Mayfair apartment flooded his mind, and the strangest urge to kiss her overwhelmed him.

Easy, Bawo! he cautioned himself.

"Would you like a head massage too, princess?"

"What did you call me?"

He shrugged, looking at her feet and trying to regain control. "Princess. That's how I see you. You're beautiful, soft, and delicate. You belong in a palace."

Amenze's mind drifted to the prophecy, leaving an unpleasant taste in her mouth.

"Yes, a head massage sounds divine." She lifted her glass to her lips, took a sip, and closed her eyes.

Bawo massaged her feet, enjoying the little sounds of pleasure she made. When he finished, he looked up and was almost certain she was asleep. Feeling mischievous, he tickled her feet, and she shrieked with laughter and jerked her feet.

"Your foot massage is over, princess," he informed her. She pouted for only a fraction of a second before laughing again.

"My head massage now, please." She shut her eyes again, evidently enjoying herself. For some odd reason, her enjoyment made him happy.

"I'm going to mess up your hair, but I'll brush it when I'm done," he whispered in her ear, and she nodded in response.

He expertly massaged her head and shoulders, sensing the tension dissolve under his skilled touch. She closed her eyes and relaxed. He could tell she was falling asleep. By the time the session ended, she was sleeping.

He whispered in her ear, "Wake up, princess."

Bawo chuckled softly as her eyes sprang open, and she turned to look at him. "So, what do you think?"

She looked dumbfounded but quickly recovered and shrugged. "It should have been longer."

"It will be longer and better when you're paying for it," he teased and held his hand to her, nodding toward the stairs. "Come on, let's do something about your hair."

It neared midnight when he pulled up in front of her flat. He switched off the engine and turned to look at her.

"Thank you for spending the evening with me. It's the most fun I've experienced in a long time."

"Thank you for having me over and for food, wine, and massages. I thoroughly enjoyed both massage sessions."

"I am certain that you did. I'm that good."

Amenze swatted his arm playfully. "Proud peacock," she teased.

"Not proud. Just very self-assured," he chuckled.

Then, as the chuckle faded, their gazes were locked on each other, rendering him speechless. In response, he leaned in and performed the one action he had longed to do since they reunited at the charity ball. He pressed his lips against hers. The moment their lips touched, it was like a detonation of passion. Literal fireworks. Just like the first time. She opened her mouth and granted him access to deepen the kiss. Her arms wound around his neck, pulling him in even as he snaked his arms around her waist and pulled her closer.

"Get rid of Dimitris. Come with me to Paris next weekend." The words were out before he could stop them. But before he berated himself, she nodded vigorously. "Is that a yes?" he whispered against her mouth. Once again, she nodded.

He walked her to her front door and entered his Jaguar to drive home. As he did, his phone rang.

"Who is this?" Bawo demanded.

"Prince Ajoritsedere Toritseju Esijolomisan Tunoka."

"I am Bawo Domingo," Bawo immediately corrected. He hated that name, and he loathed being called by the name of the man who sired him. "I know who I am. Who are you?"

"Do you know who you are, Prince Dere?"

Bawo ignored the question. He would not let this person goad him. "For the last time, *who are you?*"

"I am Mene Omaejemite, the Ologbotsere of Warri Kingdom. Or, if you like, traditional prime minister. And you are the son of Prince Eyimofe Tunoka, who became Olu Erejuwa I, twelfth Olu of the Warri Kingdom."

Bawo sucked in his breath sharply. He anticipated this day for years, but not this quickly. Thirty-three years ago, Oma Domingo, a palace maid impregnated by Olu Erejuwa I, gave birth to him. According to the diary found amongst her things, Oma's beauty enraptured the king. An affair ensued, and Oma became pregnant. Although the king tried to protect her from his jealous wife, it proved ineffective. The queen poisoned Oma, forcing her to go into labour. Aware of her impending death and desperate to protect her unborn baby, she embarked on a journey to Ode Itsekiri, where she delivered him before passing away.

"Erejuwa is not my father. What do you want?"

"I called to inform you that your uncle, Olu Ginuwa III, is ill. We fear he may not recover."

"What has that got to do with me?"

"It is time, Prince Dere. It is time to return home and take your rightful place as the Olu of Warri."

"I don't have time for this nonsense. The Olu of Warri has a son who is currently the crown prince."

"Yes. But your uncle shouldn't have been Olu. You should have succeeded your father. Now, you can take what is rightfully yours."

"Listen, Mene, or whatever your name is, Erejuwa is *not* my father. I have no business with the throne. Leave me be." He brought the call to an end.

He perceived he hadn't heard the last of the caller or the matter. The earlier he decided how to handle it, the better before it created another scandal.

CHAPTER EIGHT

As she departed work that evening and journeyed to Dimitris' apartment in Kensington, many thoughts occupied Amenze's mind. She was burdened with many things to say to him but not entirely confident on how to bring up the topic—not that she thought Dimitris would be terribly upset about breaking up with her. If Aphrodite's claims held true and Amenze found no reason for the older woman to lie, Dimitris was prepared to make an official announcement of his engagement to Elena once his relationship with Amenze concluded.

She pondered why he led her on for a long time despite the absence of any spark in their relationship. If they'd been madly in love, it would make sense why he would hold on to her for over a year, knowing Elena waited on the sidelines for him. But they weren't madly in love. He was her friend, kind, and treated her decently. Amenze wondered why she agreed to date him. She had never removed him from the friend zone, and she didn't think he'd ever seen her as anything other than a friend.

She slept in Dimitris' house with no fear that he would make sexual advances towards her. He occasionally kissed her, more on the cheek than on the lips, and when on the lips, it was chaste. When it wasn't chaste, it was lacklustre and utterly void of passion.

She compared it to Bawo's kiss that first night. It had been full of passion. And his desire was evident in his eyes as he begged her to spend the night with him. Yes, that passion overwhelmed her as she had refrained from actively dating during her undergraduate days. She had known very little about handling a man's desire and baulked.

Dimitris asked her to date him a few weeks later, and she accepted. She considered him safe—water where Bawo was fire threatening to consume her. Not that she loathed fire, but she preferred the slow burn to the inferno Bawo unleashed at their first meeting. She hoped for the slow burn with Dimitris, but it never happened.

Was Elena the reason? Did Dimitris love the woman his father handpicked for him to marry? Aphrodite gave the impression that it was an arranged marriage, but if Dimitris had not grown to love her in the year and a half that she dated him, it must mean that his affections lay elsewhere.

Amenze considered the emotions it evoked in her. She realised she didn't care. No jealous feelings existed, no anger was present, there was nothing. A bit like when she'd found out about Elena. Granted, the suddenness of it all left her in a state of disbelief, but once the initial shock subsided and she'd had time to process her feelings, she realised that she didn't care about Dimitris and Elena and their arrangement.

She'd expected Dimitris to conclude the relationship by this point, mainly as she detected his withdrawal over the phone during their few conversations following her chat with Aphrodite. However, he failed to do it, resulting in her taking on the task. After Bawo kissed her and invited her to Paris, she sensed he didn't want to be a casual friend. He wanted more. And where she would have run in the other direction over a year ago, she welcomed his desire and passion. She wanted more, too—more of Bawo. The moment had arrived to release Dimitris.

She entered the code to his house and hoped he hadn't changed it. The code worked the first time, granting her access to the building, an old Victorian-style property initially owned by Dimitris' late father and remodelled for his use in London.

A stylish three-bedroom house with a cloakroom and guest bathroom on the ground floor, ensuite bedrooms on the first, and a spacious living room and open-plan kitchen on the second.

Amenze heard Dimitris' voice as she climbed the carpeted stairs to the first floor. He appeared angry, and the person he conversed with had to be on the phone since she detected no other presence in the house.

"No! I don't want a divorce. I want an annulment!"

Amenze stopped in her tracks and proceeded no further up the stairs.

"What do you mean I can't have an annulment since the marriage was consummated? Is non-consummation of a marriage the only grounds for annulment? I can't give you any grounds for annulment. You're my lawyer. I am paying you a lot of money to get me an annulment. I can't afford a divorce. Listen, it wasn't a marriage that was meant to take place. Neither of us remembered our actions that night two years ago. We were in Vegas partying, indulging in drinks and drugs, and boom! We woke up married. And while we have continued to see each other discreetly, and I am happy to keep her on as a mistress, there has to be an annulment of the marriage. I can't officially announce my engagement to Elena while I am still married to Iris."

A pause occurred, and Amenze took another step up the stairs, her pulse quickening.

"A divorce will be messy. There was no prenup. Do you think she will walk away without a good chunk of my money? Besides, I can't afford the publicity. If the press gets wind of this, it will take a miracle for Mastoroudes to allow me to marry his daughter."

Amenze decided she didn't want to hear anymore. On shaky legs, she fled down the stairs and out of the building. Her heart raced as she hurried towards the train station.

Dimitris was married and had been for the last two years. She dated a married man for over a year. Who exactly was Dimitris Papadopoulos? Did she even know him? She wasn't sure anymore.

It was too much for her to process. She would not think about it today. She managed to push it away from her thoughts, which proved relatively easy, especially since later that night, she received birthday wishes via social media from friends living in countries where the time difference indicated that it was already her birthday.

The congratulatory messages continued to pour in through the night and early hours in the morning through phone calls, text messages and various social media platforms. She found it distracting but welcomed it. Dimitris' message was loudly absent. But after the phone call she'd overheard yesterday, she realised why. He had his hands full.

Between Iris and Elena and his eccentric sister Aphrodite, who would kill him when she discovered the truth, he had no time to think of Amenze or remember her birthday. Not that she wanted him to. He was a married man seeking to get out of that marriage and enter another. It was messy, and she wanted to distance herself from it. And to think that his sister thought she was keeping Dimitris from officially becoming engaged to Elena. She didn't even make the equation. What a laugh.

She still needed to see him and formally end things. A text message or breakup over the phone would never do. But today was her day, and she didn't want to ruin it by getting into a breakup drama with Dimitris. This evening, she left for Paris with Bawo, a free woman ready to see where a weekend with him led.

She struggled to contain her excitement all day as she imagined a weekend in Paris with Bawo. Her excitement level proved so immense that not even Efua's negativity could dampen it.

She had returned home and was packing her weekend case when Efua casually walked into her room. Amenze rolled her eyes, wishing the other woman had travelled for the weekend or removed herself from the flat and stayed out until Bawo picked her up.

"Amenze!"

Slowly, Amenze paused in front of her half-open lingerie drawer and turned to glare at Efua.

"What?"

"Snap out of your daydream."

"What?" Amenze experienced confusion. What did Efua mean? "Daydream? I am in no daydream."

"You looked zoned out!"

Amenze spread out her hands. "Maybe because I don't want to talk to you right now." She picked up some underwear and tossed them in her suitcase. "Listen, Efua, I have a lot on my mind."

"As you should if you plan to go to Paris with Bawo for the weekend," Efua sneered. "It is insane, and you are insane! You are crossing a line that you shouldn't cross. Remember that you are in a relationship with Dimitris. And Bawo is a playboy who only wants one thing!"

"And I might just give it to him this weekend!" Amenze turned on her angrily. "Yes, I am going to Paris with Bawo. Let me worry about the consequences, Mother."

"This is no time to be sarcastic." Efua sounded offended. "What about Dimitris?"

Amenze folded her hands. "What about Dimitris? You're his advocate, so you tell me. What about him?"

Efua frowned, a little confused. Amenze laughed.

"I am too busy just now to send him a Dear John letter."

"You're acting strangely."

Oh, you don't know the half of it, Amenze thought while shrugging.

"Shouldn't you wait until you've ended things with Dimitris before rushing to Paris with Bawo?"

"The relationship with Dimitris, assuming it ever existed, is already dead to me. I am certain that Dimitris shares the same sentiment. How many times has he been in touch in the last month? It's my twenty-sixth birthday today. Has he called to ask if I have plans and what they are? Efua, I am a grown woman, and I think I can manage my affairs."

Efua snorted. "I hope you know what you're doing. Bawo is a playboy and will never get married. Even if he gets married, I assure you, it won't be to you."

"Oh? And who would he marry?" Amenze sneered. "Let me ask you this, Efua: how many women have been to Bawo Domingo's home?"

"Well, I never heard that he's taken a woman there."

"So, if he took me there, surely there's hope?"

Efua's eyes widened. "He took you to his house? I thought he was taking you out for dinner. Did you visit his house?" She stared at Amenze in utter disbelief. "Are you saying you'll marry Bawo Domingo?"

"Efua, I am not saying anything. I am simply refuting your claim that he won't marry me."

And with that, Amenze continued packing her bags. "Oh, and I will send you pictures from Paris. Watch this space."

Efua left her alone then, and Amenze pulled out her phone and texted Dimitris.

Hi Dimitris. We need to talk. I am away this weekend, but can we chat on Sunday evening when I return? It's important.

A few minutes later, her phone beeped. Dimitris had replied.

Hey Amenze. Sure, we can catch up on Sunday. I am away in Greece this weekend but back on Sunday. Should we meet at your place or mine?

How about we decide when Sunday comes?

Amenze hit the send button and waited for a response. There was no response, so she put her phone away. Bawo arrived within an hour. Amenze heard the doorbell, and before she could react, she heard Efua walking towards the door.

"Hi, Bawo." Efua's voice was saccharine sweet. "Please come in."

"Hi." Bawo's deep, familiar voice reached Amenze's ears as she left her bedroom.

"Hi, Bawo," Amenze called as she walked towards him. His eyes lit up. Efua cleared her throat noisily, causing Bawo and Amenze to turn to look at her.

"I'll be in my room, Amenze." She walked away.

"Hi." Bawo pulled her into his arms and kissed her forehead. "What's all this?"

Amenze followed his gaze to the side of the room piled with flowers and cards.

"Flowers for me," she said.

He frowned. "You have many admirers."

Amenze shook her head. "These flowers are from my parents and siblings for my birthday."

"Your birthday?"

"Yes," she affirmed. "It's my birthday today."

He looked displeased. "Did you plan to tell me?"

Amenze spread her hands and grinned comically. "You know now."

They left for Paris on Bawo's private jet. Upon arrival, a team of staff from the House of Oma in Paris selected to look after Bawo's needs during his visit ushered them to their hotel. A small team comprising a hairstylist, makeup artist, and fashion stylist stood ready to assist Amenze in looking her best for the event. The fashion stylist provided a rack of clothes according to Bawo's instructions. With her help, Amenze selected a floor-length, one-shoulder evening dress in midnight blue lace and sequin fabric.

The newly constructed House of Oma Tower stood impressively on the glamourous Avenue des Champs-Élysées, and the formal opening ceremony sparkled. There was a cutting of the ribbon, a tour of the building, interviews with the press, endless photographs, speeches, dancing, lots of champagne, and canapes and just before midnight, Bawo stole her away.

"Where are we going?" she asked as he placed his hand on the small of her back and led her towards the bank of elevators.

"You'll find out soon enough," he assured her.

They travelled up to the penthouse, which housed Bawo's office. It was large enough to fit the small two-bedroom flat Amenze shared with Efua. The ceiling-to-floor windows provided a stunning view of the Arc de Triomphe, the Place de la Concorde, and the Eiffel Tower. It comprised a suite with multiple rooms, allowing him to rest, shower, and change during the workday.

Impressive, she thought. Nevertheless, that wasn't what astonished her.

A large birthday card, a gigantic teddy bear, and a salted caramel chocolate birthday cake awaited her. Amenze gasped and turned to him. When did he order all this?

"I would have been the first to wish you a happy birthday today. However, I was unaware that it was your birthday. Now that I am aware, I want to be the last to wish you a happy birthday. Happy birthday, Amenze. I hope your new year brings you everything you wish for." He gestured towards the cake.

Amenze watched, tongue-tied, as he lit the sparkling cake fountain candles. "Make a wish," he instructed with a smile that hinted at his enjoyment of her bewildered look.

She obeyed, and the clock on the wall chimed. It was midnight.

CHAPTER NINE

Bawo frowned as he prepared for his dinner date with Amenze to mark her twenty-sixth birthday. Two things troubled him: Mene Omajaemite, who had been calling almost nonstop since last night, and his relationship with Amenze.

He pushed thoughts of the Ologbotsere of the Warri Kingdom out of his mind and focused on Amenze. He needed to get a grip. Fast. The situation was quickly spiralling out of his control. He urged her to leave Dimitris and join him on this trip. She heeded his request. What next? A woman like her wasn't used to his usual arrangement. Besides, did he expect her to leave her boyfriend of more than one year for a no-strings-attached arrangement?

Bawo halted while knotting his tie and tried to gather his thoughts. It was exactly what he sought, wasn't it? Surely, he didn't seek anything different or lasting. *Or did he?* That posed the issue. He didn't know, having not fully processed his thoughts and decided what he wanted from Amenze. He desired her to choose him, to release Dimitris, and while that had its benefits since Dimitris wasn't exactly an option, now that she was free and with him, what were his intentions for her?

He had the option to be friends with her and maintain the status quo as it was, without a label, but just as rapidly as that thought entered his head, he dismissed it. That was not an option. Another man would take her away. The moment she sensed he wasn't ready to commit, she would put him in the friend zone, and he would sit and watch as another man wined, dined, and bedded her. He shook his head. No. That was not what he wanted.

Perhaps she would be his mistress. He scratched his chin, which was smooth after a recent shave. No. Amenze would never agree to wear the mistress label. Besides, he didn't keep mistresses, although he would make an exception in her case. If she would accept, it might be the arrangement that would work. They could be together until the passion in him ran out of steam. He would take care of her and gift her a house in London at the end of the relationship. He grimaced. It was probably best not to voice this line of thought to Amenze.

By the time he finished getting dressed, he remained just as uncertain about what to do with Amenze as he was when he first got out of the shower. He shrugged, satisfied that he didn't need to decide tonight or this weekend. While in Paris, he would embrace the moment and ensure she enjoyed herself immensely. He considered the dinner date he'd planned and the diamond earrings he would present to her before the evening ended. He hoped she would be pleased; he relished treating her like a queen.

Yes, he would go with the flow and show her a good time in Paris, but give her some distance when they returned to London and check in with his feelings again to see what he wanted from her. Yes. That would be the best way to go about it. Some time away from her, a little distance between them, with no contact, would help put things in perspective.

His mind shifted to the other matter bothering him. With each passing day, the call for him to assume the throne as king of the Warri Kingdom became stronger, and he could no longer afford to ignore it. Eventually, he'd have to face his destiny. He turned towards the bed as his phone vibrated. His frown deepened. Mene Omajaemite. Again.

Amenze stood in front of the mirror, unable to believe her eyes. She looked like another woman. A more beautiful, glamorous woman. It seemed as if she had walked off the fashion runway or the cover of a glamorous celebrity magazine. Her strapless, embellished, sequined silver mermaid dress flattered her figure perfectly.

She sported box braids that reached her waist with curled tips. The hairstylist braided the hair using hair extensions in a dark brown colour that complemented her skin tone. He sectioned the hair, creating a bun on her head with the top half and letting the bottom half fall to her waist. She looked great and wondered what Bawo would think.

He'd made her so happy the last twenty-four hours. She assumed her birthday celebration would end with the oversized teddy, birthday card, and cake presented to her just before midnight. But no. Bawo did nothing half-measure. He pulled out the stops today. After breakfast, his staff whisked her away to the House of Oma Tower for a pampering session in the spa while Bawo attended meetings.

He ordered everything from facials, waxing, and full-body massage to a new hairstyle, dress, and matching accessory for their dinner date tonight. She was brimming with excitement. Eki and Tiyan had unforgettable twenty-fifth birthdays thanks to their significant others, while she did not.

Her parents and brothers tried to make it memorable, giving her money so she could spend a weekend in Seychelles, and at the last minute, Dimitris bought her a gift. But her heart had yearned for a unique experience with a special someone, and she'd told herself that she was acting like a romantic fool and differed from Eki and Tiyan, who wasted their time dreaming foolish dreams.

Now, on her twenty-sixth birthday, she was experiencing the fulfilment of her dreams. However, fate proved cruel as there was no future for her with the man who granted her every wish. Amenze sighed wistfully as she sprayed some perfume on her pulse points. She may not have the future, but she held the present and intended to maximise it.

Amenze turned towards the bedside table as her phone vibrated. She smiled. It was probably her mother, calling to check on the outcome of her birthday celebrations yesterday. She hoped she would keep it short and sweet as she didn't want to be late for her birthday dinner with Bawo.

She reached for her phone and wondered where he was taking her. She had asked, but he refused to say, and she did not push, elated that he considered making the day memorable when he'd only found out yesterday.

Her phone continued to vibrate, bringing her to the present.

"Hello, Mummy." She greeted her mother cheerfully.

"Amenze, my dearest daughter, how are you?" Sisi Tuedor's voice carried a smile, which caused Amenze's smile to widen.

"I'm not only your dearest daughter but also your only daughter," she reminded her mother cheekily.

Sisi Tuedor chuckled at the remark, and Amenze imagined her rolling her eyes and shaking her head. "I hope you enjoyed your birthday celebration yesterday."

"Yes, I did," Amenze answered. She recounted to her mother the details of her activities yesterday and this morning, mentioning that Bawo would be taking her to dinner shortly.

"The instant I laid eyes on that young man, I had a strong feeling he was the ideal choice for you. Please forget Dimitris and that wretched prophecy and focus on this man. I like him."

"You have said so enough times for me to believe it, Mummy."

"And speaking of the wretched prophecy, I understand from a palace staff that Olu Ginuwa III has joined his ancestors. The unfortunate event occurred this morning, and it is top secret. It might even be a rumour, but if it is true, please make sure you tie your wrapper upside down."

"Okay, Mum, I'll remember to do that." Amenze rolled her eyes as she hung up. She would never understand the reason behind tying one's wrapper upside down when the Olu of Warri died.

The magnitude of the information her mother had shared was dawning on her. The Olu of Warri had departed to the afterlife. What did this mean for her? Surely, it meant she would marry his son, the Crown Prince of Warri, who would soon be named Olu Designate.

"Amenze, you look magnificent."

As Amenze emerged from her bedroom and entered the living area of their two-bedroom hotel suite, Bawo found himself compelled to take a step back to fully appreciate her beauty and transformation. A day at the spa made an enormous difference. He thought she was undoubtedly the most beautiful woman he had ever encountered.

As she came closer. He wound an arm around her waist and pulled her in, enjoying the scent of her perfume before pressing his lips on the soft skin behind her ears. That was all he would permit himself if they were going out for that dinner he'd planned. Also, he wasn't quite ready to take her to his bed.

"Thank you, kind sir," Amenze responded and stepped out of his embrace, whirling to flaunt her new dress and hairstyle. He approved. She looked gorgeous.

"But I think I may have cost you a small fortune," she warned.

He placed his hand over his chest as if he were on the verge of experiencing a heart attack. "Oh, no! Will I have to liquidate my business to pay the bill?"

She swatted him playfully with her silver sequined clutch bag. "Don't be dramatic," she chided and stepped closer to straighten his bow tie. "So, where are we going?"

He grinned mischievously. "After you smacked me with your purse, I will not tell you where I'm taking you. You will wear a blindfold until we arrive at our destination."

Amenze gave him an incredulous look as he sauntered off in the direction of his bedroom. "Are you being serious right now?"

Bawo grabbed the cravat he wore the night before. *This will be so much fun*, he told himself, wondering why he hadn't thought of it earlier.

"Turn around," he ordered as he returned to the lounge, where she stood and watched him in amazement.

"What?" she giggled. "What are you going to do?"

Bawo scowled in an attempt to look serious. "Amenze!"

"What?" she enquired, examining his face to gauge his level of seriousness.

"Do as you're told, Amenze," he warned.

Still smiling, she turned around, and he delicately slid the silk cravat over her eyes and fastened the knot at the back of her head.

"And this is for swathing your arm."

"Yes," he whispered in her ear. "I need to teach you to be more respectful." He was on the verge of laughter.

"Okay, Bawo. I will play along, but if you have ruined my hair or makeup with this stupid stunt of yours, I will kill you!"

"Did you just say stupid? And did you threaten to kill me?"

She tensed momentarily, wondering what he would do next. Then she angled her head towards him. "Yes, I did. What are you going to do?"

"I'm going to do this," he announced and, without warning, tickled her. He chuckled as she began to wriggle and laugh uncontrollably.

"Bawo! Stop! Get away from me, you wicked man!"

Bawo shook with laughter. "Come on, let's go, or we'll never make it to dinner."

Inside his tuxedo pocket, his phone vibrated, and his heart skipped a beat. He pulled it out and stared at the screen. It was Mene Omajaemite. He slipped the phone back and willed himself to focus on Amenze. Tonight revolved entirely around her.

He slipped his arm around her waist and turned her around to face him. "Do you trust me?" He smiled as she nodded without hesitating. "Good. Leave the blindfold on. I'll be your eyes for now."

She nodded again as he took her hand and led her out of the suite. As they arrived at their destination, Bawo leaned across in the limo's back seat and removed the blindfold. Amenze looked about her and then at Bawo, who watched her silently.

"The Eiffel Tower?" She laughed softly. "We're having dinner at the Eiffel Tower? You've got to be kidding me, Bawo. Get out of town!"

"While 'get out of town' wasn't the exact wording I was aiming for, the reaction is spot on," he teased.

*****

The experience proved to be thrilling for Amenze as they rode up in the glass lift to their restaurant. On the only previous occasion she had been to Paris, she had glimpsed the Eiffel Tower but hadn't set foot inside. This presented an entirely new experience for her. The view of the Paris landscape took her breath away. Knowing they would have that view as they dined and be able to see the hundreds of tourists milling around the old Paris monument added to her excitement.

As they waited to be shown their table, Amenze excused herself and headed to the bathroom. She wanted to ensure that Bawo hadn't ruined her hair and makeup, and she also wanted to text Efua. She'd continuously texted Efua and provided her with updates since they arrived in Paris yesterday. Perhaps Efua

122

would stop pestering her about how unsuitable Bawo was for her.

Bawo couldn't be more suitable for her. He had swept her off her feet and given her a romance she once wrinkled her nose at and not because she didn't want it, but because she thought it only happened in the novels and movies and real men were incapable of genuine romance.

It seemed unjust that after this experience with Bawo, life would drag her away to be another man's wife. Thoughts of the prophecy made her wonder if Bawo had heard any rumour of the Olu of Warri's death.

So, as they were busily tucking into their dinner, she asked, "Have you heard of the death of the Olu of Warri?"

To her amazement, Bawo choked on his food and coughed, instantly putting down his cutlery and picking up his glass of water. Amenze stared at him wide-eyed, wondering at his reaction. But of course, he would react that way. He was an Itsekiri man with a natural allegiance to his king, even though he hadn't lived in Warri for years.

She leaned forward and covered his hand with hers. "I am sorry for blurting out the question like that. It was thoughtless of me. Because I am only half-Itsekiri and on my mother's side, I always forget or take for granted what matters to the average Itsekiri person."

As Bawo regained composure, he feigned a smile to put Amenze at ease. Inside, his heart was racing, and more so as the phone in his breast pocket vibrated as if on cue. He could swear it was Mene Omajaemite, and if there was any truth to the words Amenze had spoken, he knew why Mene was calling. Something told him he would see Mene in person soon. He took a deep breath.

"From my reaction, you know I was blissfully ignorant of the death of the Olu. How did you hear, and when did he die?"

"I got a call from my mother just before we left the hotel. She says it's currently top secret, but a palace staff told her he died earlier today."

"I see. Here's to his son, the next Olu of Warri." Bawo lifted his wine glass and hoped Amenze did not notice the slight shaking of his hand as their glasses clinked.

The ride back to their hotel was quiet. Bawo appeared to be in deep reflection. His phone also kept buzzing, and it seemed to annoy him as he clearly did not want to speak to whoever was calling. Eventually, he turned it off. Amenze did not understand his mood. Besides, she had thoughts of her own. The old Olu she had feared was her husband had died, and it was now clear that she would marry his son, a younger man, instead.

With no knowledge about the Crown Prince of Warri Kingdom, she couldn't help but wonder about his personality. Despite her desire to google him and see his looks, she restrained herself. She was in Bawo's company; it was neither the time nor the place. Also, what did it matter how he looked? He was a total stranger to her. She was not any more thrilled to hand him her virginity than she'd been to hand it over to his aged father. She would give it to Bawo, she decided there and then. It was their last night in Paris. What better way to end their little weekend getaway?

So, as they stepped into their suite, Amenze pulled him close.

"Thank you for making this weekend and my birthday memorable. I love all my presents - the teddy bear, diamond earrings, and spa day. You know how to show a girl a good time, Bawo."

She reached up as Bawo leaned down and covered her lips with his. As the kiss became heated, Bawo pulled away.

Amenze whispered against his mouth. "Stay with me tonight."

Bawo sighed, and she could see the strain on his face. "Amenze, I know what you're about to do and trust me, it's a bad idea." He kissed the top of her head. "You get a good night's sleep, and in the morning, we'll talk."

Ignoring him, Amenze clutched at his tux lapels and attempted to pull him closer for another kiss. But he grabbed her hands and gently pushed her away from him. She blocked his exit as he tried to move past her toward his bedroom.

"Amenze, please, help me. I am hanging by a very thin thread…"

Before he finished, she had moved into his arms, and he was kissing her against his better judgement.

CHAPTER TEN

What had he done?

Bawo stared in utter horror at the tiny but distinct spot of blood on the white cotton sheets. He looked from the stain to Amenze's naked body lying next to his and felt instant mortification. He put his head in his hand and groaned. Finally, this woman had driven him to damnation. He had crossed a line he should never cross and put a nail in his casket.

He got out of bed instantly, pulled on his trousers, and moved to his bedroom. He would shower quickly and return to run a bath for her, which would help with her soreness.

You complete idiot! He scolded himself as he quickly showered. *What have you done?*

He had slept with a virgin. He could not believe it. Any moment now, he would awaken and realise it had been a terrible nightmare. He closed his eyes under the spray of warm water and opened them again. Nope! It was real. Very real. As real as Amenze lying naked under the sheets in the adjacent room, and might he add, no longer a virgin. That was wrong on so many levels. He had slept with many women but never touched an inexperienced woman. He seethed with anger at himself.

How could he have been so stupid?

He had assumed that because she had a boyfriend, she was having sex constantly. Well, if not constantly, but she'd had sex before. Not once in his wildest dream had he imagined her to be a virgin. How was she a virgin, anyway? Was Dimitris impotent? A eunuch? This was such a mess! Sisi Alero repeatedly told him as a young boy that a virgin wasn't to be touched unless he intended to marry her. As he grew into adulthood, he had made it his personal rule to avoid virgins, and he had just broken it.

Was he out of his mind?

As for her, what trick did she think she was pulling by withholding this information from him? Why did she throw herself at him like that? He certainly had not been expecting that. It had caused his body to stir in a way that it had not since, well, since whenever. And now this. Did she have any anticipation of a marriage proposal? She wanted to be married. Her friends were all married. Without a doubt, she had preserved her virginity for marriage, and now she had given it to him without disclosing the full extent of what he was getting involved in.

The proper thing would be to marry her. He knew this, but he rejected it. No woman would pressure him into marriage. As a young boy growing up in Ode Itsekiri, he witnessed many fights between married couples. He observed married men drown their sorrows in alcohol. He witnessed more of it when he moved to Europe. In his brief life, Bawo had seen men's visions ruined by the women they married out of pressure and a sense of obligation arising from sex.

Bawo decided long ago to only marry when he chose and whom he wanted. To ensure he gave no woman a chance to manipulate him, he sought arrangements with experienced women who knew that marriage wasn't on offer. He was a big spender and prepared to give lavish gifts, but a wedding ring wasn't one of those gifts.

Amenze differed from the women he usually moved with, and it contributed to his attraction for her, but he wasn't so taken with her that he would marry her because he had taken her virginity. Marrying her should be his decision, not something he did because he had no choice. He detested being put in a difficult position, and that is exactly what she accomplished by allowing him to sleep with her without informing him of her virginity.

He recalled the moment he deduced her inexperience. He tried to pull back, but the seductress chose that minute to wrap her legs around him and urge him on. Without a doubt, she was well aware of what she was doing. Did she plan from the beginning to tempt him into taking her virginity and then manipulate him into feeling obligated to marry her? She was about to discover that a man like him wasn't easily manipulated.

He could hear his phone ringing. The person calling him at this late hour had better have something important to say. He turned off the shower, grabbed a huge fluffy towel, and rubbed himself briskly. Before answering the call, he slid on a pair of pyjama bottoms.

"What do you want from me?"

"*Ale je efun ooo!* The earth has eaten the native chalk. Olu Ginuwa III has joined his ancestors, Prince Dere. You are required to return to Warri and take your throne."

"Not on your life, Mene! I promised myself long ago that I would never sit on Erejuwa's throne!"

"Prince Dere, I want you to consider what your mother would have wanted for you and herself."

"Leave my mother out of this! Don't you dare mention my mother! And stop calling me Prince Dere and stop calling me altogether. Sod off!"

He tossed the phone away and walked off to run Amenze's bath.

*****

Amenze sighed and looked out the window as Bawo's private jet took off toward London, leaving Paris behind. As dusk approached, the aerial view of Paris held a captivating beauty, but she gazed upon it in the hope of finding a more fulfilling pastime. Bawo sat across from her, engrossed in his laptop. She might not have been there for all the attention he spared her.

He had been pensive all day, attending meetings and ignoring her. It was almost like he regretted sleeping with her. This seemed strange because once he had overcome the initial surprise of discovering her virginity, he had cherished her body in a manner she had never imagined. And the look in his eyes, she could have sworn she'd seen it many times. It was the same way Oba Osad looked at Eki, the same way Usi looked at Tiyan, Sato looked at Ede, and her father looked at her mother. The way she'd hoped Dimitris would look at her, but he never did.

And afterwards, he had been very tender. She had slept off wholly exhausted after their lovemaking, only to be awoken by him just before he picked her up and carried her into the bathtub, a bath he had run for her.

"It will help with your soreness," he'd whispered in her ear as he held her tenderly in the tub, his powerful hands gently stroking her body. It had been bliss. They'd stepped out of the tub and made love again before giving in to a deep sleep, their arms wrapped around each other.

But this morning, he had changed. Become an entirely different man. She had woken up to find him gone, and her heart had sunk as she'd looked from the space beside her where his body had lain during the night to the tiny but distinct blood stain on the sheets. A part of her body and evidence that she was now a woman. She had felt a cloud of sadness descend.

As a little girl, her mother had taught her the importance of saving herself for the man she married. While she didn't build castles in the air or dream of Prince Charming like Eki, she'd known for most of her life that she wanted to save herself for a man she loved and who loved her back. She thought she was falling in love with Bawo, and when he made love to her, she thought he may also be falling in love with her. Yet now she recognised her mistake.

Waiting for them as they landed in London was the same black Range Rover and driver who had dropped them off a few days ago. The ride to Amenze's house was just as quiet as the flight. Amenze half expected him to remain in the vehicle when they arrived and was taken aback that he got out with his driver to help with her bags and giant teddy bear.

As Amenze unlocked the front door and entered the living room, she raised a hand and flicked the light switch. A man sat in the armchair in the corner of the room. Bawo, who closely followed behind her, did a double take.

"Dimitris?!"

"Dimitris?!" Amenze was shocked to see Dimitris in her home. She'd made an appointment to see him but had not asked him to come to her flat!

Had Efua let him in? Why would she when Amenze had not returned from her trip? And why did he sit in the dark and wait for her return like a stalker?

Bawo's driver discreetly put down her teddy and bags and exited the flat, shutting the door quietly behind him. Amenze felt Bawo's arm encircle her waist and draw her closer as if to show Dimitris that Amenze was now with him or perhaps to imply to Amenze that he was right beside her and she didn't have to handle Dimitris alone. Amenze leaned into him. Dimitris stood up slowly, unfolding his six-foot frame from the chair, and didn't miss the gesture.

"So, this is what you've been up to in my absence, *Agape mou?*"

Amenze remained unaffected. "Why are you here, Dimitris? Why didn't you inform me you were coming? And why were you sitting in the dark, waiting for me to get home?"

Dimitris pushed his hands deep into the pockets of his suit pants. "So many questions, but I think I should ask the questions here. My topmost question is, what are you doing with Bawo Domingo? If I find out that you've been cheating on me with this—"

"Enough, Dimitris!" Amenze spat out. "You've been doing enough cheating for both of us. Our relationship ended as soon as I heard about Elena."

"You know about Elena?" Dimitris scowled at Bawo.

"Yes!" Amenze said. "Your sister ensured I did. If it were just Elena, that would be fine. But there's also Iris!"

Dimitris glanced from her to Bawo and back to her. "You know about Iris?!"

His eyes grew narrow. He looked almost dangerous. Amenze exhaled as Bawo's protective arm around her waist tightened.

"Yes, I do. Please don't ask me how or what I know. I am not interested in repeating it to you or anyone else. But you have no moral justification for being in my house waiting for me to return from Paris with Bawo, so you can accuse me of cheating on you."

Dimitris swore slightly under his breath. "*Agape mou*—" he began.

Amenze held up her hand. "Please don't call me that ever again. I am not your beloved. And I need you to leave now."

Dimitris stared at her for a long time, sighed in defeat, and ran a hand through his thick black hair.

"Okay, I will go, but I must tell you, Amenze, stay away from him." He peered at Bawo with contempt in his eyes. "He is not good for you."

"Please leave, Dimitris," Amenze looked away, fighting back the tears. Dimitris had been her friend; they'd had some good times together, and it hurt her that they wouldn't remain friends.

As Dimitris turned towards the door, he paused by Bawo. "I told you she was different, and I meant it. If you hurt her, you worthless swine, I will kill you. And in the future, stay away from me and my sister. You come close to either of us, and you are a dead man."

Without waiting for a response, he walked out of the flat, leaving Amenze alone with Bawo and a reeling head.

Amenze looked at the shut door and sighed, rubbing her temple. She could feel the beginnings of a headache. It certainly had been one of those days.

Once Dimitris left, Bawo put some distance between him and Amenze. He seethed with rage and made every effort to conceal it. Once again, his reputation had been tainted. And he remembered clearly that he had tried to avoid it by asking Amenze to get rid of Dimitris before coming to Paris with him. When she proceeded on the trip, he assumed the boyfriend issue had been resolved. He made a mistake. Judging by the brief scene only moments ago, she had not ended her relationship with Dimitris as he had requested.

"Instances like the one that just occurred are not my cup of tea. That's precisely why I asked you to get rid of the boyfriend before joining me in Paris."

He watched her massage her temple. It was the second time she'd done that in the space of a few minutes. Was she feeling unwell? He longed to go to her but kept himself rooted to the spot as he waited for her response.

"Believe me, Dimitris and I were done when I came out to Paris with you."

He tried to make sense of her explanation but failed. "I see. Well, apparently, he didn't get the memo and probably because you didn't bother to tell him."

Amenze wrapped her arms around herself and shrugged, or maybe her shoulders trembled slightly. He wasn't sure. He waited for her to speak and proceeded once it was clear she wouldn't.

"There's something else bothering me. Would you care to explain to me how you happened to be a virgin when you dated Dimitris for more than a year?"

"I never slept with Dimitris," she muttered quietly in response. She was dying inside and just wanted him to leave and not witness her breakdown. And she was close to breaking down.

"Well, that's obvious." He nodded.

Amenze felt so ashamed she couldn't bring herself to look at him.

"And why is it that you didn't sleep with Dimitris?"

"Call me old-fashioned, but my mother constantly told me when I was a little girl to save myself for the man I marry."

Bawo remained silent for a while. So, he had been right. She had been saving herself for marriage. "I see." He did see. "Which brings me to my next question. Why me, Amenze? You threw yourself in my arms last night. Why?"

Amenze pondered how to respond. Her heart sank by the minute. She wanted him out of here so she could lick her wounds in private. This wasn't how it had been for Eki, who'd recklessly given her virginity away to Oba Osad the first night she met him. Here she found herself, after three weeks of getting to know Bawo, being cross-examined and treated with no more respect than a whore.

When she didn't answer, Bawo continued speaking.

"What did you hope to achieve by giving me the gift you should keep for your husband? Marriage? Well, I have news for you, Amenze. There will be no marriage. Bawo Domingo is not the marrying kind and doesn't fall for the schemes of manipulative women."

Amenze fought back the tears. "You have made yourself abundantly clear. Please remove your unwanted presence from my home."

Bawo had no intention of staying a moment longer. He was done here and finished with her. When he said there'd be no marriage as compensation for the lost virginity, he meant it. He could return to his life now that the difficult situation was over. So why didn't he feel the thrill and excitement of freedom as he walked out of her house and into his waiting vehicle?

CHAPTER ELEVEN

As Bawo entered his home, he could hear his house phone ringing. He hurried up the stairs and toward his home office. The caller ID revealed it was Suf. It was also 1 a.m. What did he want? He frowned as he lifted the receiver to end the persistent ringing.

"This had better be good, Suf," he growled.

"Please, Bawo, tell me that after all this brouhaha, you will marry this woman."

His frown deepened. What was the meaning of this? "Suf, what are you talking about? What brouhaha?"

"You haven't seen the publication in your favourite online magazine."

Bawo powered up the laptop on his desk. He typed his name in Google, and his eyes widened as pictures of him and Amenze taken during their dinner at the Eiffel Tower came into his sight.

What was this? The paparazzi had followed them on their dinner date. Why? He understood that the news magazine was interested in his love life, but what intrigued them about Amenze? He saw a picture of her with Dimitris next to a picture of them together while he gave her the diamond earrings. The angle of the photo concealed the box's content, making it appear as if it were a ring.

The caption he read alleged he had stolen Dimitris Papadopoulos' girlfriend. He continued to read. They accused him again of having an affair with Oba Akran's fiancée and mentioned that despite his reputation for pursuing women in relationships, this time, it seemed like he was genuinely in love and marriage was imminent.

In love? Did he appear to be in love? Bawo examined the photo carefully, instantly feeling disgusted by his intense gaze into Amenze's eyes. Angrily, he snapped the laptop shut. He had seen enough!

"Please, tell me that after this stir you have caused, you are considering marrying her," Suf said.

"God forbid," he countered. "I don't do the ball and chain. I told you that."

"Bawo, did you hear me?"

"I heard you, Suf. I am not deaf."

"Think about the merger deal, and please tell me you are considering marrying this young lady."

"Neither you, the business or some online newspaper will force me into marriage. I will marry who I want when I am good and ready, and not one moment before. If Chez Aboh thinks my reputation is so bad he can't do business with me, he isn't ready for business and can go to hell with the deal."

"And the young lady? What's her name, Amenze?"

"Yes. Amenze. She will be fine."

"Will she?"

Bawo slammed his hand on the desk.

"She is a grown woman, and I never promised her marriage. Mind your own business and stay out of my private affairs, Sufyani."

*****

Amenze cried all night. At dawn, she felt unwell and too miserable to go into the office. She called the office, cancelled all her appointments, and attempted to work from home, making phone calls and responding to emails.

About noon, she got a call from Ede, who had been in London for a few days to attend to some business concerns and left for Benin that night. Ede had gone to her office to surprise her and take her to lunch but learnt that she was working from home.

As they chatted on the phone, Ede sensed from Amenze's voice that something wasn't right.

141

"Are you okay, Amenze?" Ede sounded worried. "You don't sound like your usual cheerful self."

"I am fine," Amenze tried to convince her but failed woefully. She was very near to tears, and her voice showed it.

"I am coming over," Ede announced and ended the call.

Ede arrived an hour later, looking effortlessly chic in a red designer tailored suit, matching pencil skirt, and black Ralph Lauren suede pumps. Her long, permed hair, styled in a sleek bun and bangs, completed the business look.

Next to her, Amenze looked grim in her dusky pink lounge sweatshirt and shorts set. Over her braided hair, she wore a pink satin hair bonnet.

"Hey, Amenze, it's so good to see you." Ede stepped into the flat, put her bags on the wooden console table by the door, and gathered Amenze into her arms.

Amenze was so overwhelmed that she broke down and cried, telling Ede in incoherent words how she had slept with Bawo and broken up with Dimitris. Ede squeezed her tight.

"It's going to be okay, baby girl, I promise," she crooned like one would to a little child.

Ede arrived with Chinese food, which she threatened to force-feed Amenze if she didn't behave and eat of her own volition. She made Amenze sit in a giant beanbag, sauntered into the bedroom, where she'd been working on her laptop up to that moment, and took the duvet off the bed. She brought it to Amenze and tucked it gently around her.

"Do you want your laptop?"

Amenze nodded. "Yes, please."

Ede immediately headed to the bedroom, fetched the laptop and brought it to Amenze. "Are you comfortable?"

Amenze nodded in response. She worked on her laptop for a bit as Ede took the food into the kitchen to heat it and serve it on plates. She returned and handed Amenze a plate and a long glass of orange juice before settling on the couch with her food and drink.

Seeing her made Amenze happy. Right now, she needed a friend. She didn't feel at ease discussing last night's events with Efua. Efua would show no sympathy and eagerly say, "I told you so."

Amenze tried some of the sesame prawn toast and acknowledged their deliciousness. "Thank you for lunch, Ede. This is delicious."

"Anything for you, baby girl." Ede placed her plate on the coffee table and sipped her drink. "I had to see you. And I am glad I did. I have missed you, and it's so good to see you."

"It's good to see you, too, and you are positively glowing. Marriage becomes you. How is Sato doing?" Amenze still didn't understand how Ede could leave Sato for days to attend to her business in London.

Ede's eyes lit up. "He's fine. I miss him terribly, and we've been apart less than a week and have spoken on the phone at least twice daily. But it's not the same as being in the same location. I can't wait to be back home tomorrow. My flight arrives in the early hours of the morning. Hopefully, I can catch him in bed before he wakes up."

"Oh, please!" Amenze rolled her eyes and grumbled simultaneously to show she didn't need that level of detail, and Ede laughed good-naturedly.

"Soon, dear girl, you'll know what it's like." Then she waved a hand dismissively, flashing her diamond engagement ring and wedding band as she did. "But I'm not here to talk about me. What's happening to you, baby girl? You sounded awful on the phone. You gave me a scare."

Amenze could understand why. She had always been the stable one among her friends, able to maintain her composure while they were becoming frantic. Now that she was a mess, they naturally couldn't believe it and were worried.

Amenze sighed. How had she been so foolish and wrong about Bawo? For the nth time since yesterday, she asked herself the question. They'd had a strong connection. She'd felt it. Meeting one's soulmate was a foreign concept, but with Bawo, she thought she'd finally met her true soulmate. She wasn't naive to believe there wouldn't be conflicts. She fought with her best friends, parents, and brothers. But they didn't leave each other's lives because of heated arguments and disagreements. They stayed together, caring for each other and working together to resolve the issues.

Had it been too much to expect of Bawo? Had it been too much to expect that when disagreements arose, they would work it out together? Yes, he felt angry about her not informing him about her virginity. But she hadn't meant to deceive him deliberately. Furthermore, at what moment during their conversations was she expected to have mentioned, *hey, Bawo, I'm a virgin*? Also, she hadn't known it would be such a big deal for him to sleep with a virgin, or she would have told him. She presumed he was a playboy, delighted to jump into bed with any woman desirable and willing.

He desired her. Her mother had seen it the first time she'd met him. Besides, the desire had been unhidden and unbridled the first time she'd met him. He had also not put up much resistance when she had seduced him. Why did he have to continue as if she'd committed a sacrilege? It was the twenty-first century, and she wasn't expecting a man to marry her simply because he had deflowered her. Moreover, her destiny was to marry the Olu of Warri.

"What's going on?" Ede twirled her fork and eyed Amenze attentively. "All that crying and rambling earlier on. What was it about?"

Amenze sighed again and placed her plate with the half-eaten contents on the coffee table. Where did she begin?

"Do you love him?"

"Love who?" Amenze jerked up her head suddenly to look at Ede. To whom was Ede referring? Was she even following her at all?

"Your Greek god of a boyfriend," Ede responded with a wink as she sipped her orange juice. "That's what this is about, right?"

Amenze released her breath. Ede had not been following her. It wasn't surprising. She'd been crying a lot while talking, and Ede assumed she was heartbroken over the breakup with Dimitris. She would share the story once more.

Starting at the beginning, she told Ede about Bawo and how he'd swept her off her feet. She explained about Dimitris and Elena but not Iris and clarified that it had not been Dimitris who'd broken her heart but Bawo. She'd made an awful mistake and given herself to a man who had zero plans to commit to her and thought she was a manipulative woman out to wring a proposal from him.

"Oh, Amenze," Ede put a hand over her mouth in shock. "I am so sorry to hear this."

Amenze shrugged as she reached for her plate. "I guess we can't all have love and the happily ever after. I can't say I will ever find the spark you and Sato have." She bit into a sweet and sour chicken, chewing slowly and allowing herself to savour the taste.

"Don't say that." Ede shook her head vehemently. "It's not true. You will find someone you love and who will love you in return. Sato and I didn't always have a great relationship. There were many times I thought he hated me and that I had lost him forever."

Amenze recollected that Ede had experienced a stormy, roller-coaster relationship with Sato despite their powerful chemistry. Sato acted like he didn't care when he was always hopelessly in love with Ede.

"But it worked out in the end, and now you're both so happy," Amenze reminded her before taking another bite of her food.

Ede had a dreamy look in her eyes as she lifted her left hand and studied her engagement and wedding rings as if she still couldn't believe she was married to the man she loved.

"Yes. We are happy. Joyous! And I believe you will be, too. You will meet someone right for you."

"Hmm…" Amenze reflected as she chewed her food. "I may have to move to Warri for that one. The great chief priest, Usi, said I would marry the Crown Prince of Warri Kingdom."

Ede nearly choked on her drink. "What? He can't be serious! Did I never tell you about my experience with the Crown Prince of Warri Kingdom?

"Well, now that I think of it, you mentioned your father wanted you to marry him."

"Yes, he did," Ede told Amenze the whole story, including how Prince Jimi had laced her drink with an aphrodisiac so he could sleep with her. She watched as Amenze's eyes widened in shock. "How good are Usi's predictions?"

"I would say pretty good. Eki ended up with the Oba of Benin, even when she tried to escape him."

"So that means you have a future with Prince Jimi." Ede sighed. "Well, people change."

"Indeed, they do," Amenze muttered, sipping her drink and cursing the rotten luck that seemed intent on matching her with a man with a negative reputation. Then she paused as she considered what Prince Jimi's reaction would be upon discovering she was no longer a virgin.

"What's wrong, now?" Ede queried as Amenze looked sad.

"I have given myself to another man. My chances of marrying the Olu are even slimmer now. With Olu Ginuwa III, I didn't care if he rejected me because he was old, and I didn't want him. But this is a much younger man. If he is the one and I have blown my chance…"

Ede shook her head vehemently. "You think that because you're not acquainted with him. Prince Jimi considered my virginity archaic. He said it made him feel mediaeval when my father informed him I was a virgin." She burst out laughing, and Amenze joined her.

"Well, he's a weird one."

Ede nodded. "You don't know the half of it." She took a bite of her spring rolls. "Come back to Benin for a while. I will arrange for you to meet Prince Jimi. Sato can't stand him, but we can do this without getting Sato involved."

"I will come to Benin soon; I need a break. First, I must be in London to host Elevate's first pitch event in the diaspora."

"Ah, that's right. I had completely forgotten about that. How's the preparation for that coming along?"

"We're on track to holding a very successful pitch event. This will be better than the maiden edition in Benin months ago."

"I am confident that you will succeed. I'll be waiting anxiously to hear all about it." Ede put down her drink and rummaged inside her tote bag for her iPad. "Let's get you a flight booked for the day after the pitch event."

Amenze did not get an opportunity to change her mind. They spent the next half an hour looking at flights and finally booked Amenze's flight to Benin for the day after the pitch event. Ede left for Benin that night. Both women hugged, kissed, and promised to catch up in Benin in two weeks.

CHAPTER TWELVE

"Sod off, Sufyani. Tell Chez Aboh to go to hell. No one tells me what to do. This is my ship. Should I go to HR and get a document proving my ownership?" He raised his head from his laptop and glared at Suf.

Suf grinned and shifted his body weight back and forth between his legs. "That won't be necessary, Bawo. I am well acquainted with such a document."

Bawo glared at his laptop screen and continued working, expecting Suf to leave. When he didn't, he scowled at him. "Well, what now?"

"You're in love with her, aren't you?"

The question caught Bawo off guard, and for a moment, he was tongue-tied. "You are crazy, Suf. Get back to work. And that's an order."

He looked back at his screen, but he could see nothing. Suf chuckled softly, and when Bawo glowered at him, he immediately pulled a straight face before heading towards the door.

At 3 pm, Bawo decided he'd had enough for the day, as he was still in a foul mood and unable to focus. Chez Aboh could go to hell along with the deal. He didn't need it. He would focus on his existing spas and making luxury goods for women. The customers who bought his products didn't care about his Casanova reputation.

His mind drifted to Amenze several times, but he suppressed his thoughts. She could go to hell, too. He realised he had failed to use protection both times he'd made love to her. Suppose she got pregnant? Well, if she did, he would provide for his child. There was absolutely no doubt about that. But he would not marry any woman simply because she was pregnant. She should have considered pregnancy before seducing him.

He struggled to concentrate, and in frustration, he informed Emami of his intention to leave early and asked her to reschedule his meetings. At home, he attempted to continue working from his home office. He sat in a high-backed fabric armchair in one corner of his office, next to the drinks cabinet, his feet propped up on the matching footrest. Before long, he started drinking, quickly finishing his favourite brandy. And then he became inebriated. And then he fell into a slumber.

As Bawo stirred, he instantly became aware that he was not alone because his gaze fell on a pair of red shoes.

Was he dreaming?

Standing before him was a tall, dark man, possibly about his age, dressed in a pristine white *Kemeje*, the traditional Itsekiri long-sleeved collarless shirt. He wore it over a white silk George wrapper, gathered in pleats around his waist and falling superbly to the ground around his feet. Tied in opposite directions around his waist were two long red satin sashes, the same shade as his red suede designer shoes and the same length as his wrapper. The heavy red coral beads around his neck and wrists told a tale of his affluence.

Before Bawo locked eyes with the intruder, he was confident of who it was. Chief Mene Omajaemite. The Ologbotsere of Warri Kingdom.

"What the hell—?"

Unsteadily, Bawo stood up. Mene pushed him back into his seat by placing both hands on his shoulders. Two elderly men in similar attire, presumably palace chiefs, stood behind Mene. His gaze shifted towards the digital clock on the wall. It was 8 pm.

"What are you doing in my house? And how did you get in?" Bawo demanded, standing unsteadily again to his feet. "Better have a good explanation, or I'll call the police."

"Sit down, Prince Dere. I am here on urgent royal business. The king has joined his ancestors, and I have no time for the antics of fools."

"Did you just call me a fool?" Bawo growled. "When I am your king, you will cease to be Ologbotsere."

"If you agree to be king, I will gladly step down as Ologbotsere," Mene retorted. "It would be a tiny price to pay to give your father, my late Olu, his final dying wish."

Bawo scoffed, "I do not care about Erejuwa's dying wish. And I do not wish to fulfil it. Erejuwa was not my father!"

Mene rolled his eyes and sighed simultaneously. "Here we go again!" He sounded exasperated. "You keep saying that Olu Erejuwa I was not your father, but you have failed to correct me by telling me who sired you. So it must be that Olu Erejuwa I was your father, and you know it. You know also that you were born for the throne, or you wouldn't dare use the title Ogiame in that club of yours. Oh yes, we have heard."

"It is just a moniker. It means nothing." Bawo shrugged.

"It is not a moniker. It is the sacred title reserved for the Olu of Warri. In using it, you were daring the kingdom, daring Itsekiri sons and daughters to challenge your use of the king's title. You knew no one could challenge you. And that begs the question, why won't you be king? Why do you continue this senseless game? Why do you continue to deny your father, your birthright, and your throne?"

Bawo remained silent. He could not think of a response. It had to be that drink. He had had too much to drink. It was all Amenze's fault. Damn her. Mene took advantage of his silence and carried on. He was on a roll.

"You know you are king. Your uncle, Olu Ginuwa III, should never have been king, but you never came forward. Those who knew of your existence couldn't find you, so your uncle was crowned king. And when we find you, instead of manning up and coming forward to claim your birthright, you deny it—content to play games and crown yourself Ogiame thousands of miles away from Ode Itsekiri.

"If you are Ogiame, act like it and quit fooling around already. We are pressed for time. Your uncle is dead. The council is determined to replace him with his son, Prince Jimi. For your sake, we have not proclaimed the Olu's death to Itsekiri sons and daughters. Come home and take your place and marry and fulfil your destiny. Enough of sowing your wild oats in the white man's land and disgracing your heritage."

"I have not in any way disgraced my heritage."

"I beg to differ, Prince Dere. I am aware of what the trash magazines say about you. For someone who constantly denies being Olu Erejuwa's son, you resemble him very much where it relates to women."

"Yes, I do. Don't I?" Bawo smirked. "So, you can say that I am not disgracing my heritage, but my actions align with my heritage. Erejuwa would be proud, wouldn't he?"

He should be. He had loved beautiful women and sired many daughters with many concubines.

"Enough, Prince Dere. Please sit down, and let's chat like reasonable men." Bawo turned in utter disbelief to look for the owner of the voice. The man, dressed in traditional Benin attire, was on the screen of a laptop sitting on Bawo's desk. He was sure it belonged to Mene. The image quickly moved to the gigantic TV screen mounted on the wall opposite Bawo's desk. It seemed Mene had made himself at home.

"Well, I guess there's no need to ask you to make yourself at home at this stage," he mocked as he dropped back into the armchair and propped his feet on the footstool.

Mene ignored the jibe and turned to Oba Osad, who filled the screen and looked so imposing he might as well have been in the room with them. The chiefs who accompanied Mene took the two armchairs on the other side of Bawo's desk, and Mene remained standing next to Bawo's chair.

"Thank you for joining us in this meeting, Your Majesty," Mene addressed Oba Osad. "I will begin by bringing Prince Dere up to speed."

Oba Osad put up a hand to halt Mene. "Thank you, Chief Mene. But before you do that, it's only proper that we introduce Prince Dere to the other royal fathers joining this call."

Bawo frowned as several other men appeared on the screen. He instantly recognised Obi of Agbor, Chez Aboh, the Oba of Lagos, Sijuade Akran, and the notorious self-proclaimed King of the Niger Delta, Tamuno Donokoromo.

He groaned as he thought of his current relationship with the Obi of Agbor and the Oba of Lagos. This would be a long meeting. As if the Oba of Benin read his mind, he intervened.

"Whatever has happened or not happened in the past, between you and my brothers, it is now in the past. You are Prince Dere, born to sit on the Warri throne, and that makes you one of us, a fellow royal father and brother-in-arms. Our code permits no misunderstandings between us. Do I speak your minds, great kings?"

"Indeed, you do," Chez Aboh immediately replied.

"You do," Sijuade Akran concurred before looking straight at Bawo. "All is forgiven, brother."

"And in case you're wondering what this means for the business deal. It's a yes. We're going forward."

Bawo's lips curved upwards. This was good news. He couldn't wait to tell Suf.

"I am pleased that we're proceeding with the merger, but if you're doing it to make me take Erejuwa's throne, it will not happen."

"We will get to that part soon. Let's not be hasty," Oba Osad suggested. "You are acquainted with the Oba Sijuade Akran and Obi Chez Aboh. Please allow me to introduce the King of the Niger Delta, Tamuno Donokoromo. Popularly called Tam Dono."

"I have heard of you, Tam Dono, although we have never met," Bawo said. He turned and addressed Oba Osad. "Is there a reason they're all here?"

"The presence of every king here is to assure you we are behind you and won't rest until you take your rightful place on the Warri throne. And we will do what it takes. Even if it means fighting dirty."

That would explain the presence of the King of the Niger Delta, a militant known for being a loyal friend but a menacing adversary. There was no limit to what he would do to retaliate against his enemies, even resorting to kidnapping. He possessed great wealth from the extensive oil deposit in the Niger Delta and fought oppressive West African governments on behalf of the poor, oppressed, and downtrodden.

"And that is why Tam Dono is here?" Bawo asked.

"Yes," Oba Osad replied. "He will make disappearances happen if need be."

Bawo raised a brow. "Yeah? And who will be disappearing?"

"Prince Jimi Tunoka," Tam Dono answered promptly as if he had been anticipating the perfect time to do so. "And anyone else who needs to disappear."

Bawo supposed that the list consisted of Prince Jimi's mother, sisters, and cabinet chiefs loyal to the late Olu of Warri. He groaned and buried his head in his hands.

"Don't worry about any of that right now," Oba Osad advised him before addressing Mene. "Chief Mene, it is probably time to bring Prince Dere up to speed."

"Yes, Your Majesty." Mene bowed slightly towards the screen and turned to Bawo. "Prince Dere, just before your father, Ogiame Erejuwa I, joined his ancestors, he asked for an audience with his brother-in-arms, the Oba of Benin, Oba Edoni. He told Oba Edoni about you and asked him to search for you. His search for you through your mother's family had reached a dead end."

"This is nonsense. Why would Erejuwa look for me on his deathbed? My aunt took me to him before my first birthday.

He told her I couldn't be the child he fathered with the palace maid. At eight years old, she took me again. Again, he said I wasn't his son as I looked nothing like him. Then, at sixteen, just after the death of my aunt, I presented myself to him, and he taught me a lesson to ensure I never returned. On his orders, palace guards stripped me down to my underwear, held me down, and flogged me. Twenty-four lashes by a palace guard. I never forgot. I never returned to him. And I never will. Erejuwa is not my father. If I reject him, it is only because he first rejected me."

The entire room fell into silence. The four kings, Mene, and the chiefs appeared motionless. Undoubtedly, this part of the story was new to them. Erejuwa had not shared this tiny detail. How could he tell anyone a mere palace guard had flogged his son, who would one day sit on his throne? It was inconceivable.

"Whatever your father did to you, Prince Dere, I can assure you, he regretted it. The knowledge that he was dying having never bonded with you, the knowledge that he would never know the joy and pride a father feels when he holds in his arms the son who would one day succeed him… I think that was sufficient punishment. That his brother, instead of his son, sat on his throne, whether for a day or five years, was his judgement from the gods. It is time to put that aside and take what is rightfully yours," Mene said.

"You keep saying that, and you keep calling me by this strange name that Erejuwa gave me, and yes, he gave that name to the child my mother was pregnant with, but when he set his eyes on me, he said, not once, not twice but thrice that I was not the same child. Not his son."

"True," Oba Osad interjected. "But as Chief Mene has said, he regretted it. He told my father he was disappointed because you looked nothing like him. He said every time he looked at you, he saw your mother. But if he'd spent time with you, he would have realised that you are exactly like him on the inside, and anyone who has ever met him only needs to sit with you for a while, and they will see the same mannerisms. You even have the same voice. I met your father several times growing up, so I know."

"How did you all find me? I have never used the names Erejuwa gave me before my birth."

The names had been in his mother's diary, but his aunt Sisi Alero had chosen not to draw unnecessary attention to him, especially since his father had rejected him. She had called him by the last word his mother had spoken before her death. No one knew whether his mother had meant for it to be his name or if she had been making a declaration. Nevertheless, it became his name and was shortened to Bawo, and he adopted his mother's surname. Thankfully, he didn't look like Erejuwa, so he'd grown in obscurity far away in Ode Itsekiri.

"Finding you wasn't too hard," Oba Osad responded. "My father looked for you here in the United Kingdom because your father mentioned you had left Africa." A relative of your mother's, although she did not know your paternity, had come forward when your father began to look for you and mentioned that a Portuguese member of the Domingo family had taken you with him to Europe. She also said your name was Bawo Domingo. Once my father had that information, he asked questions.

"This had to be done carefully, not to alert your uncle to the possibility that he wouldn't be Olu. Just before my father joined his ancestors, your business, House of Oma, came to his attention. Unfortunately, he could not do any investigation, but he left me a letter. It took a while before I found the letter, and I needed Chief Mene's support before pursuing the matter further. My bodyguard employs a team of well-trained ex-military men and women and with you carrying on as Ogiame, their job was simple. The DNA test with your uncle confirmed that you are indeed your father's son."

Bawo frowned. "What do you mean DNA test?"

"A sample of your DNA was extracted from a drinking glass you used at the club," Oba Osad said.

Bawo's frown deepened. "Who is responsible for this?"

Only when Oba Osad moved his screen did Bawo see the tall, dark, and stoic man standing behind the Oba. That was the bodyguard? The man responsible for getting a sample of his DNA? The man who had breached his security?

He turned to Mene. "How did you get into my house?"

Mene remained silent, but his eyes revealed the truth as they shifted towards the screen. In anger, Bawo sprung to his feet and walked towards the TV. He put his face close to the screen and bellowed menacingly at Sato.

"When I find you, you are dead!"

To his satisfaction, Sato took a step backwards. Oba Osad turned to look at his bodyguard.

"*Vbo sunu?*" he rebuked him in the Benin language. "What is the matter? The man's far away, on the other side of the world!"

"I am not *the man*. Please address me properly, Oba Ubinitie." Bawo moved away from the screen.

"What was that?" Oba Osad demanded. "What did you call me?"

Bawo turned to Mene and grinned. "Mene, enlighten him."

Mene cleared his throat. "Your Majesty, *Ubinitie* in Itsekiri means small Benin."

Oba Osad looked at Bawo long and hard and then chuckled softly. "I like you," he decided and looked at Mene. "I really like him."

Bawo grinned. "You're not too bad yourself, Oba Ubinitie."

Oba Osad nodded. "And now, you'll need that smart mouth to convince the council of chiefs to make you king in your father's stead."

"Or not." Bawo shrugged and dropped into the armchair. "I have heard all you have said, but it doesn't mean I want to be king."

Oba Osad turned to address Mene. "Chief Mene, hand him the letter from his father." Then he addressed Bawo. "We will bring the meeting to an end. Chief Mene and his entourage will remain in London for another meeting with you."

"And if I still refuse to be king?"

Oba Osad shrugged. "Between Sato's efficient Bulwark guards and the King of the Niger Delta, I am sure we'll be able to get you to Ode Itsekiri in time for your coronation." He grinned as Bawo instantly looked horrified. "But it hasn't come to that."

"And I am certain that it won't." Mene passed a letter to Bawo as the kings logged out of the virtual meeting.

CHAPTER THIRTEEN

Bawo pushed back his swivel chair and rose to stare out of the ceiling-to-floor window of his twelfth-floor office in the heart of London. He should have seen the city's beautiful sights, including The River Thames, Tower Bridge, Big Ben, The London Eye, and The Shard, but he saw nothing.

It was all as void and gloomy as he felt inside. The past two weeks without Amenze had been a struggle. He had lost interest in most things. Most nights, he dreamt of them still being in Paris, with her lying beside him. Yet, as he tried to touch her, she disappeared, and he opened his eyes to the awareness that Amenze was not in his life anymore, and the feeling of emptiness that followed was indescribable.

He had grown accustomed to texting her constantly. Sometimes, he instinctively reached for his phone before bed, only to remember Amenze's absence, leaving him with extreme sadness and longing.

Last night, Emami accompanied him to the Chamber of Commerce dinner and awards ceremony. She was a much safer option if he desperately needed a companion. He requested her company to avoid misunderstandings about his intentions with a potential date and because he worried about Amenze seeing him photographed with another woman.

During the dinner, he thought he heard Amenze's distinct laughter, and instinctively, he spun toward the sound, and the disappointment on his face was hugely visible. Without saying a word, Emami reached under the table and tightly squeezed the hand resting on his thigh. He had not told her about Amenze. He rarely discussed his private affairs with Emami, but as his private secretary, she saw, heard, and knew while acting as if she didn't.

After the dinner party, he'd returned home, and once more, Amenze featured in his dream. He'd made love to her repeatedly, and then, just as the dawn approached and he reached for her, he realised it had been a dream. He occupied his super king-size bed alone. His heart sank, and he detested his solitary way of life for the first time. The townhouse had always been a sanctuary, his private space where no one was allowed. It was for this reason he'd bought the Mayfair apartment. There, he did all his entertaining, but when it was time to be alone, he retreated to his private space and never noticed its cold emptiness until now.

This morning, he showed up early to work, trying to distract himself like he had done the last two weeks. However, with each passing day, it became increasingly difficult, and today, he refused to be distracted. His desire was for Amenze. He wanted to talk to her again, tease her, laugh with her, and make love to her. Yes, he wanted all those things.

Two weeks had passed since the night they returned from Paris, giving him ample time to ponder the matter and reach a conclusion. He missed her and was convinced he didn't want a fling, not with Amenze. He wanted something longer. Marriage still bothered him; he wasn't ready to take the plunge, but he could ask her to try living together for a few years, maybe have a kid or two.

Convinced he knew what he wanted from her and confident he could make her settle for cohabitation in the interim, Bawo left his office in search of Amenze. He was intentional about leaving his pride behind. He was ready and willing to beg, grovel, and do whatever it took to get her back, back in his life, back in his home, back in his bed.

He showed up at her office, hoping to take her to lunch. However, he was informed that she was out of the country, and the receptionist refused to disclose her destination. He called her mobile phone, and it was switched off. There was a sudden settling of dread in his chest. He returned to work irritable and unable to focus, and he snapped at the long-suffering Emami several times before the end of the workday.

That evening, after work, he drove to her house, hoping her flatmate, Efua, would give him some information. Efua opened the door and let him in before announcing, "She's not here."

"Where is she?"

"Well, she's gone where she should have gone weeks ago." Efua shrugged. "Probably already in Benin trying to fulfil some stupid prophecy."

"What do you mean?"

"She's returned to Benin. She left last night. Her friends plan to introduce her to the Crown Prince of Warri, whom she's prophesied to marry."

Bawo's heart thundered in his chest. "She's prophesied to marry the Crown Prince of Warri?"

"Yes. About two months ago, she was informed she would become the Olori of Warri Kingdom."

Amenze was going to be Olori? Absentmindedly, Bawo scratched his head as he recalled their first meeting. He'd known there was something different about her from the first moment he'd seen her. He had pursued her as he had never pursued another woman, and he couldn't understand why because she looked nothing like the women he usually favoured. Now he understood why he'd been drawn to her.

"So, she's gone to be introduced to the Crown Prince of Warri?"

"Yes. He will soon be Olu of Warri."

She had gone to marry Prince Jimi. But Prince Jimi would not be Olu!

And why not? You don't want your throne! His inner voice sneered. He shut it down and turned to leave, surprised when Efua stood in his way.

"Where are you going?" Efua stood on the balls of her feet and wound her arms around his neck. "Why are you in such a hurry? You only just got here."

Bawo tried to stay calm. "I have a meeting at The Dorchester."

"Will you come back?" She slowly stroked his shoulders.

"Why do you ask?"

"I thought we could spend some time together. I could make you some Ghanaian jollof rice. Suf told me once that you enjoy it. And you could stay over. Or I could come to your house."

"Women are not allowed in my home."

"But you took Amenze there." Efua pouted.

"And does that bother you, Efua?"

"Of course it does." Efua sounded frustrated. "Bawo, she's hardly your type. You and I should be together. Now that Amenze's out of the way let's not waste any more time. I want you. I have loved you since that night at Kojo's charity ball." She wound her arms around his neck and tried to kiss him.

Bawo slowly removed her hands and stepped away from her. "What do you want from me, Efua?"

"Anything you're willing to give me, Bawo. It doesn't have to be marriage. I'll happily be your mistress—"

"Mistress?" Bawo snorted. "You know nothing about me. I have never had a mistress, Efua."

As she looked at him in surprise, he continued. "I make arrangements. Arrangements for a woman to accompany me when I go out and be in my bed if I so desire. Is that what you want, Efua? To be my no-strings-attached arrangement?"

"If that's what you want, Bawo, I'll take it. I love you so much. I do. And I didn't mean to do the things I did. I was jealous. I was so jealous, Bawo."

Bawo looked at the young woman, whom, for Suf's sake, he would only see as an errant little sister. He listened to her, held her as she cried, and gave her his handkerchief to wipe her tears. Then, he left the flat, more determined to get to the one woman who inspired him to want more. His earlier plan to enter cohabitation with Amenze was thrown out the window.

If there were a prophecy that Amenze would be Olori of Warri Kingdom, she would not settle for being his live-in lover and baby mama while he contemplated marriage. He needed to decide two things now. One, he would be king. No man would take his throne and use it as leverage to marry the woman he wanted. Two, he would marry Amenze, and the earlier, the better, before he lost her. If Amenze wished to be the Olori of Warri, she was stuck with him and would be the Olori to his Olu.

He had kept Mene waiting an entire week. Well, the wait was over. He sought Mene out at The Dorchester Hotel and announced his decision to be king. If his change of mind surprised Mene, he did not show it but acted like he'd expected this to be the outcome following the earlier meeting. And it might very well have been.

Having read his father's letter, it would be impossible for him to refuse the sincere apology from a dying man consumed by remorse and regret for rejecting his only son. He was asked to contact Chief Temi Jacdonmi, the Iyatsere, or traditional Defence Minister of the Warri Kingdom. The older man who had been appointed under Olu Erejuwa I held specific properties in trust for him.

Mene and his accompanying chiefs left for Warri that night. Their purpose was to announce the Olu's death officially. In a week, Bawo would join them to be formally introduced as the son and heir of Olu Erejuwa I.

He wouldn't watch Prince Jimi claim his throne and, to add insult to injury, marry his woman. Bawo intended to take what was rightfully his—the throne that was his by birth and the woman that was his by prophecy.

*****

"Amenze, I did not know you had it in you to be so reckless. I must be a bad influence on you!" Eki teased after Amenze narrated her whirlwind love affair with Bawo Domingo.

"Eki!" Tiyan chided. "This is neither the time nor place to say such things. You can see she is heartbroken. Consider her recent challenges with Dimitris' deceit and the smooth-talking Bawo. Despite all that, she successfully organised Elevate's inaugural pitching event in the diaspora." Tiyan sat beside Amenze on the two-seater sofa in the queen's private sitting room, put an arm around her and held her close. "Pay no attention to Eki, you hear me?"

"I was only teasing." Eki pouted, and when Tiyan glowered at her, she grinned like a Cheshire cat. "I am sorry, Amenze. I didn't mean to be insensitive."

Amenze beamed at her best friend to reassure her. She knew her friends loved her and how glad she was to be back in Benin with them. It was her first meeting with them since her arrival yesterday morning.

Ede looked up from her iPad. "Our priority right now is to devise a strategy to bring Amenze and Prince Jimi together.

"Yes!" Eki said excitedly. "And since you are already acquainted with Prince Jimi, we'll leave that to you."

Tiyan frowned. "Hey. Hold it there, ladies." She turned to Amenze. "I thought you said my husband told you not to make this happen?"

Eki rolled her eyes. "Tiyan, please, we are aware that Chief Usi Isekhure is your husband, but please, for the duration of this meeting and while we are talking about the prophecy, could you just refer to him as the chief priest?"

Tiyan made a face and looked at Amenze. "Did the chief priest say you shouldn't do anything to make this happen?"

Amenze nodded, but Ede protested. "It's just a small meeting. An introduction. She goes to his home for lunch or dinner, and they talk. Should Chief Priest Isekhure's prophecy hold true, Prince Jimi will proceed accordingly. Right?" She turned to Eki for support.

"Right!" Eki concurred and glared at Tiyan. "We aren't asking her to propose on bended knees."

"Or even mention the prophecy," Ede added.

"Precisely," Eki said.

Tiyan wagged a finger at both Ede and Eki. "I don't like this one bit. She should remain in her father's house and let the gods do their thing."

"How will Prince Jimi ever find her in her father's house?" Eki asked.

"I don't know, but when Usi gives a prophecy, it is the exact word of the gods."

Eki sighed. She could not argue with that. "But we are not trying to make anything happen. We're just suggesting bringing together two people destined to wed. The gods will have their chance to do the rest."

Tiyan looked at Amenze in resignation. "You can do it if you want. But I don't like it."

"You don't have to like it," Eki replied. "Keep silent, and don't tell your husband, the chief priest."

"We don't discuss his work very much these days, to be honest," Tiyan responded dreamily.

"You're compensating for pre-marital abstinence."

"Eki!" Ede chided, looking scandalised. "What a thing to say!"

Eki snorted. "You and Sato are just as bad. Don't let me get started on you."

They all laughed as Ede held her hands up in mock surrender. "Okay! Okay! Go easy on me, Eki!"

Ede pulled out her phone to call Prince Jimi.

"Why do you still have his number, anyway?" Eki teased her.

"Good question," Tiyan joined in. "There will be trouble if Sato finds out."

Ede grinned. "Trust me, Sato will not be the least bit perturbed. He knows he has worked his voodoo magic on me and written his name on every inch of my body. I won't be looking at any man until I die." She giggled as Tiyan and Eki gave an exaggerated scoff that showed they were teasing her.

Amenze smiled as she watched her friends. They were all so happy in their marriages. Would she ever experience such happiness? She'd experienced some happiness with Bawo but had no future with him. Her future, it seemed, was with Prince Jimi. Once again, she cursed her rotten luck.

"Hi, Jimi!"

Amenze dragged herself out of her internal monologue to look at Ede; she wasn't the only one. Tiyan and Eki were also looking at Ede with anxious expressions plastered on their faces.

Amenze had to hand it to Ede; she was a smooth operator and knew exactly what to tell Prince Jimi. She expressed her condolences on the loss of his father, which had only been officially announced that morning, and congratulated him on his becoming king. She was exceptional at playing to the gallery and Amenze listened with keen interest as she praised Prince Jimi and assured him that Warri would enjoy peace and stability under his reign.

She mentioned Amenze without taking a break or catching her breath. She told Prince Jimi that Amenze sought to meet him in person to commiserate with him on the passing of his father. To remove any suspicion on Prince Jimi's side, Ede cleverly lied that Amenze had asked for an introduction previously to discuss some business with him. She mentioned Amenze's work for Elevate, including the just-concluded pitch event in London.

She told Prince Jimi that because Amenze's mother was Itsekiri, she sought to include the Itsekiri people in Elevate's scope. Hence, she wanted to meet him in person, but as he was mourning, she sought to commiserate with him and become an acquaintance, hoping to have a business discussion when he became king. That did the trick. An appointment was made for Amenze to dine with Prince Jimi in his home in Warri in a few days.

"You are one smooth operator, Ede," Eki muttered as Ede ended the call.

"I would have believed every word she said if I didn't know better," Tiyan stated.

"A bad habit I picked up from my father, but it has its uses." Ede turned to Amenze. "It's all set up. How do you feel?"

"Nervous," Amenze admitted.

"Oh, please!" Eki sounded exasperated. "What's there to be nervous about? Have a drink for Dutch courage if you must. This is your future you're fighting for, girl. I can't wait for you to join us on the married side of life!"

"Perhaps Eki can recommend to you what she was drinking for Dutch courage the night she met Oba Osad at The Dorchester," Tiyan muttered dryly.

Eki threw a cushion at her in mock outrage, and everyone laughed.

Everyone except Amenze, who smiled faintly. How could she laugh? Her problem was a lot bigger than anyone thought it was. To her friends, all that needed to happen was for her to meet with Prince Jimi and boom! Something magical would follow. He would get on bended knees and propose marriage, she would accept, and they would live happily ever after.

But what about the baby she feared may already grow in her womb? What did she do about that? Her period should have come yesterday, but it hadn't, and while it was not the first time it had not come on the day it was expected, it was the first time she had reason to worry.

Marrying a man, having lost her virginity to another, was one thing, but marrying him while pregnant with another man's child was an entirely different kettle of fish. She wondered if the gods factored this in when they chose her to be Olori of Warri. Perhaps the baby was the very thing that made the prophecy fail.

She couldn't tell her friends she feared she might be pregnant. She couldn't tell Prince Jimi; if she was pregnant, she couldn't tell Bawo. He had called her a manipulative woman. She *would not* tell him. If she *was* pregnant, she would deal with it alone. Perhaps forgetting the prophecy and returning to London to focus on her doctorate and Elevate would be the way forward.

She would have to live elsewhere. Her father would support her; she knew that. He loved her so much that it was scary sometimes to see the lengths he would go to give her the things she wanted. She was her daddy's little girl—she had always been. Her mind went back to their conversation last night.

She'd told him about Bawo and what transpired between them. He'd listened quietly, attentively, and let her finish. Not once had he interrupted her or blamed her. Amenze hated to disappoint him, and she'd said as much.

"You are not a disappointment, my darling," he'd assured her. "You've always been level-headed. Don't worry; this isn't the end of the world. It's one mistake and can be fixed."

He'd studied her carefully before speaking again. "Have you decided what to do if you become pregnant?"

Amenze had furrowed her brows as the reality of not using protection was put before her. She'd thought over it several times since the incident and wondered how she could have been so foolish.

"If I become pregnant, I will keep the baby," she'd said in a voice that allowed no argument. Knowing her father and his line of work, she would not put it past him to suggest that she could abort the baby if she didn't want it.

Her father had pulled her into his arms and kissed the top of her head. "Your mum and I are here to support you. I am certain your brothers will take the same position. Whatever you decide, if there's a baby on the way, you won't be alone. You and your child will be well looked after. Even if I must keep working until the day I drop dead."

Realising he was teasing her, Amenze playfully poked him in the ribs with her elbow and smiled as he chuckled. She was grateful for her parents and older brothers, who always had her back. She knew her father would work until his death to ensure she and her baby, if any, never starved or lacked necessities. Her father held her in his arms, just like when she was a scared little girl. She knew then that everything would be fine.

CHAPTER FOURTEEN

Dinner with Prince Jimi Tunoka, the Crown Prince of Warri Kingdom, was not going well, Amenze concluded as she forced herself to eat the meal before her while politely asking him questions about himself. He was in love with himself and could not help talking about himself. She listened politely, but all the time, she was comparing him with Bawo.

Was he the one she was prophesied to marry? Had the gods also mentioned a divorce to Chief Isekhure, and he'd neglected to tell her? She could never be with this man. This man could never love her. This man could love no one. He was too in love with himself to have the capacity to love another human being.

Thus far, Usi Isekhure had not failed where a prophecy was concerned. He was the revered mouthpiece of the gods. If he said it, it happened. Eki had done everything to make the prophecy for her and Oba Osad fail, but it hadn't. Perhaps she was overthinking this. She came here to meet the man destined to be her husband. What happened next was not in her hands. And like Ede had said when they discussed Prince Jimi, people changed.

"You are not eating, Amenze. Is the food not to your liking?"

Amenze smiled up at him. He was changing right before her eyes. She had branded him self-absorbed, but he wasn't so self-absorbed that he hadn't noticed she wasn't eating, which was another matter. The food looked delicious, but she feared throwing up all over the table if she ate the wrong thing. She felt nauseous. It had been the same this morning.

That had led her to go into her father's clinic next door and take a pregnancy test. It had returned positive. She had told no one. And she knew the doctor she'd seen would not breathe a word. Her pregnancy was putting her off food. But she could hardly tell Prince Jimi that she was with child, could she? The only thing left to do was smile, eat, and pray that the food stayed down.

"The food is completely to my liking, Your Highness," she assured him, glancing momentarily at her barely touched plate of boiled plantains and owo soup. "I had a late lunch, so unfortunately, I am not very hungry."

He regarded her as he dabbed the sides of his mouth with a napkin. "It appears that you are not usually hungry."

Amenze knew he referred to her flat tummy and tiny waist. Though they gave her the perfect hourglass figure men loved, many wondered if she intentionally starved herself to attain it.

"What are your plans for the Itsekiri people when you become king?" She hoped the question would take his attention off her.

It did. His eyes lit up, and he talked like an orator who loved the sound of his voice. Amenze tried not to drift off in her thoughts but to smile and nod appropriately.

She attempted to eat a little to ward off any further questions but realised it had been a mistake.

"May I be excused? I need to powder my nose." She stood and stepped to the right of her chair as she spoke.

He smirked and put down his fork. "You are so English in manners." The sarcasm was evident in his voice. "But, of course. She will escort you to the ladies." His words were enough to summon a maid who stood next to her promptly.

Amenze waited for the nausea to fade, realising it was time to abandon the prophecy and embrace her new life as a single mother. While Prince Jimi may not have cared that she had lost her virginity, any man would care that she was coming to him carrying another man's child.

Besides, it didn't have to be a life of single motherhood. She could always fall in love again and marry in the future.

Amenze decided she was done trying to fulfil a prophecy. She did not know how she would be Olori, nor did she care. It was time for her to return to London and get on with her life.

After bidding farewell to Prince Jimi, she drove back to Benin and, as she dragged her exhausted body up the stairs to her bedroom, she gave her parents, who were downstairs eating dinner, a look that said she did not wish to be disturbed. Or talk about her date. Especially that. It had been a disaster. She was still far from becoming Olori despite her journey to meet the man she was destined to marry. Prince Jimi had not acted like he was interested in her. There was no mention of seeing her again, let alone a proposal. Besides, she was pregnant.

In her bedroom, she undressed and donned a green silk pyjamas shorts set as she got ready for bed. Her mother burst into her room, and she looked away from the mirror in her bathroom, where she stood cleaning her face.

"Mum, I want to be alone," she grumbled.

"Amenze, put on the television. You need to hear this." Her mother reached for the television remote on the bedside table and switched the set on. "It's an official announcement from the palace of the Olu of Warri. A young man claims to be Olu Erejuwa's son."

Amenze eyed her mother suspiciously, wondering why she was bubbling with so much excitement. She strolled into the bedroom, eyes glued to the television screen. The Ologbotsere of Warri Kingdom was addressing reporters and saying that the long-lost son of Olu Erejuwa I, Prince Ajoritsedere Toritseju Esijolomisan Tunoka, had been discovered. Amenze frowned. Who was this person? And what did this mean for her? How did it affect the prophecy?

A picture of the newly discovered prince filled the screen, and Amenze's hands flew to her mouth, muffling an involuntary gasp.

"Bawo Domingo!"

"Do you understand why I wanted you to see for yourself? Didn't I tell you I knew he was right for you?"

Amenze felt breathless suddenly. Bawo was the son of Olu Erejuwa I? But he said nothing. He gave no sign that he was royalty. She shook her head. No, he had given two signs. She had only not been paying attention. He admitted that his moniker at his club was Ogiame, and the night they'd had dinner at the Eiffel Tower, his reaction to the rumour that the Olu was dead had been a sign. Amenze groaned.

"What is wrong?" Sisi Tuedor asked.

"I just remembered his reaction to the rumour that Olu Ginuwa III had joined his ancestors," Amenze said. "He almost choked on his food when I told him!"

"Why did you tell him? Did I ask you to spread the news? Did I not say that it was top secret? The information was for your consumption alone!" Sisi Tuedor put her hands on her head. "*Mo ku ren*! I am dead! This child, you will not kill me. I didn't kill my mother. The Olu's death is not a topic for dinner conversation!"

Amenze exhaled wearily. "I am sorry, Mum. I realise now that was a huge mistake."

"That's okay. Let's leave it in the past where it belongs and focus on the current news. Now that Bawo might be king, what does this mean for you?"

Amenze took the remote control from her mother and switched off the television.

"Mum, please, I need to go to bed." She was so close to tears that her mother did not argue. Quietly, she left the room.

Amenze climbed into her bed, assuming the foetal position as she cried herself to sleep.

*****

Bawo could not relax as he was driven to Prince Jimi's residence with Mene by his side. It was now a week and a day since he had agreed to be king. Mene and the chiefs with him had wasted no time returning to Warri to proclaim the death of Olu Ginuwa III. Bawo had watched the ceremony live.

In keeping with tradition, Mene had broken three symbolic pots containing white native chalks, one after the other, dropping them on the floor. After each session, he announced, "*Ale je efun ooo*! The earth has eaten the native chalk!"

Immediately, thirteen cannon shots followed. Thirteen signifying the number of Olus that had reigned so far. It had been a solemn moment for Bawo as he watched. The Warri Kingdom was now without a king and awaited its fourteenth Olu.

Bawo arrived in Warri that morning and immediately went from one meeting to another, speaking with chiefs loyal to his father. They all pledged their allegiance to him and declared that, as the only son of Olu Erejuwa I, he was the crown prince and the rightful heir to Olu Erejuwa's throne.

A press conference had been held to publicise his existence, and Mene thought the Itsekiri sons and daughters at home and abroad had greeted it with mixed feelings.

He did not care about that—he did not care about any of it. He just wanted to see Amenze. Before leaving London, he instructed Mene to find her, and only moments ago, he was informed that she was at Prince Jimi's home having dinner.

Bawo saw red. They instantly left the palace in an entourage of chiefs and Bulwark guards. He hadn't even bothered to change from his traditional attire.

"If she finds you attractive, she'll find him equally attractive," Mene broke the silence as their vehicle exited the palace's main gate. "You're both handsome. But you're taller, and women typically prefer taller men."

"Is this supposed to make me feel better? Or what is your point exactly, Mene?"

Bawo seethed the entire journey. Mene should have allowed him to seek Amenze earlier; this would not have happened. But he insisted they meet with caucus chiefs first and introduce him as Erejuwa's son. He wasn't sure if it was a good move, but one thing he knew: if Prince Jimi touched his woman, he would take him apart limb by limb.

Prince Jimi had been forewarned of their visit, and when they arrived at his home, they were met with hostility. Prince Jimi came out to meet them with guards of his own. Mene explained they were palace guards loyal to the crown prince and his father.

Bawo decided he would restructure the entire palace guards after his coronation. He didn't need men loyal to his uncle and cousin guarding him. Currently, his security was provided by Bulwark guards. Bulwark was owned by Sato

Ihaza, the Oba of Benin's bodyguard and friend, and Mene assured him that he could trust every one of them. As Sato had refused to offer Prince Jimi Bulwark's services, Bawo was greatly reassured.

"Get off my property!" Prince Jimi barked at them before turning to look at Bawo. "I don't give a damn who you are! Don't come into my house throwing your weight around."

"I have no intention of staying or throwing my weight around. Give me my fiancée, and I will be on my way," Bawo responded.

He had not asked Amenze to marry him, but referring to her as his fiancée felt right.

"Who is your fiancée? Amenze?" Prince Jimi quizzed. "She came to see me of her free will and didn't tell me she belonged to anyone. Get off my property. I will not tell you again!"

"I am king. Technically, I own the piece of land upon which I stand. Didn't you learn in school that all of Warri belongs to Ogiame? *Ale Iwere ti Ogiame!*"

Prince Jimi glanced between Bawo and Mene. "Is this the nonsense Mene has been feeding you?" he demanded. "If it is, it is a shame because it implies he is ignorant of Itsekiri customs and traditions. And if you have swallowed it, you are even more ignorant than he is. You are not king. You cannot be king. My father was the immediate past king; his throne is mine."

"The throne is inherited vertically, from father to son, not horizontally between siblings," Bawo informed him. "Your father sat on the throne that was rightfully mine. The gods rejected him from the start. You will never be king."

Prince Jimi turned to Mene. "You betray my father like this? May I remind you it was my father who made you Ologbotsere? And this is how you repay him, by bringing some impostor to take his throne from his son?"

"Prince Dere is not an impostor. He is the son of Olu Erejuwa I. Your father may have appointed me Ologbotsere, but he was only carrying out the wishes of Olu Erejuwa I. Besides, I am an Ologbotsere descendant, so it is nothing out of the ordinary that I was appointed Ologbotsere. As for who becomes king, it is entirely up to Ife, and *Okparan-umale*, the chief priest, will make it known shortly."

Prince Jimi, still enraged, glared at Bawo. "You cannot have the throne any more than you can have the woman who brought herself to my home. She strolled into the lion's den. She is mine for the taking, and I intend to have her tonight."

Bawo lost his last shred of sanity and dignity. "I am going to kill you!"

He lurched forward, his head connecting with Prince Jimi's face. Immediately, palace guards and Bulwark guards rushed forward, and there was pandemonium as the guards became entangled in their battle as each group tried to extricate its boss. Fortunately, Mene called a time-out.

After the commotion, the truth surfaced that Amenze had since left for Benin. So, they returned to their vehicles and began the hour-long drive to Benin. Between Mene and Bulwark guards, they found her home even before they entered the city.

Bawo did not know what to expect upon his arrival. He had met Amenze's mother once but did not know much about her. Amenze's dad he had never met. Had she told them about him? Did she claim he was a man who had taken her virginity and might have made her pregnant, only to accuse her of being manipulative? He shifted uncomfortably in his seat.

If he thought the reception at Prince Jimi's house had been hostile, it was worse at Amenze's.

"I don't care if he is the Itsekiri king. I am not Itsekiri, my daughter is not Itsekiri, my house is not on Itsekiri land, and I want him to leave now!"

Bawo removed his Stetson and wearily ran his fingers through his faded skin haircut.

If it were up to Amenze's father, there would be no meeting with her today or any other day. But the man was mistaken. Bawo didn't travel from London just to be turned away by one person. It would take more than one man to keep him from seeing Amenze tonight.

The only positive was that Amenze's mother was unaffected by what he had done. As soon as they arrived, she ushered him, Mene, and the four palace chiefs into the living room. Bulwark guards hung back outside. It was clear she was happy to see him. She expressed her joy at learning that he was the son and heir of Olu Erejuwa I. She explained she had watched the televised announcement and invited Amenze to do the same.

That part had him worried. He had never mentioned his connection to Erejuwa and the Warri throne. What would Amenze be thinking? He realised he had much explaining to do. He only prayed that her father would let him see her. Judging by the excitement with which her mother received him, he knew she would allow him to speak with Amenze. He hoped she could influence her husband to her way of thinking.

"Dr Giwa-Amu, you need to go back to the clinic. Don't you have a pregnant woman in distress to attend to?" She turned to Bawo and Mene. "My husband is a consultant gynaecologist with a clinic next door, and he works all kinds of odd hours, always ready to help pregnant women. The clinic never sleeps, and neither does he."

"Yes, Amenze told me." Bawo addressed Dr Giwa-Amu directly. "She speaks highly of you and is proud of the work you've done and still do."

The older man appeared tongue-tied, so Bawo proceeded. "Sir, I realise I didn't behave like a gentleman towards your daughter, but I genuinely care for her and have honourable intentions; otherwise, I won't be here tonight."

Sisi Tuedor responded with glee. "Oh, this is wonderful news. The prophecy is unfolding beautifully before my eyes. My daughter is going to marry the Olu! I will be Olori's mother!"

"Woman!" Dr Giwa-Amu instantly called his wife to order. "Stop this nonsense at once! Whatever his intentions, we don't know whether our daughter wants to marry this man. And I will not let her be bamboozled or railroaded into a marriage she doesn't want, not even if she is pregnant! I will take care of her!"

"Dr Giwa-Amu, please, you will not marry your daughter. Her husband is here to take responsibility for her. Please let him go up and talk to her."

"He is not talking to my daughter tonight. She came home exhausted and uninterested in speaking to anyone. He can come back tomorrow. That will give me time to talk to Amenze and determine whether she wants to talk to him."

Bawo's heart sank. He couldn't bear waiting another day to see Amenze. Fortunately, Amenze's mother shared his sentiments.

"Dear Dr Giwa-Amu, please return to your clinic and patients and stay out of a lovers' quarrel. Is your daughter the first woman to fight with the man she loves?"

The man that she loves?

Bawo didn't have time to ponder the statement, as Sisi Tuedor was already turning to him.

"My Olu, please go upstairs; her room is the third one down the hall. The door should be unlocked." She positioned herself to block her husband from trying to follow.

Bawo did not need a second invitation. "*Do*, Sisi," he said in appreciation and nodded slightly to Amenze's father as he made for the stairs.

"*Do san gbe re!* It shall be well with you, my king! *Ogiame suooo!*" Sisi Tuedor called after him.

As he ascended the stairs, he could hear Dr Giwa-Amu telling his wife that she had acted like a foolish woman, and then Mene's soft voice tried to calm both husband and wife down.

He entered the room, and Amenze was in a foetal position on the bed, her arms wrapped around herself.

My wife, Aya mi. He spoke the words in his heart as he lay on the bed beside her and pulled her into a spooning position.

He was uncertain of her reaction upon waking to find him there. She would probably be mad. But he refused to let that worry him now. He was where he had ached to be for days, lying next to Amenze, holding her in his arms. She was his and would not be taken by any man. Not Dimitris Papadopoulos, Prince Jimi, or her father, Dr Giwa-Amu. She was his woman, and he would take care of her.

Just then, she sniffled, indicating that she must have been crying before she slept, and he pulled her closer.

"*Aya mi,* I am sorry. I was scared. I was a coward. But not anymore. I promise."

CHAPTER FIFTEEN

"Bawo?"

She couldn't be dreaming, could she? Amenze asked herself as she stirred. No, she wasn't dreaming. She couldn't see his face, but she was lying in a man's embrace. It felt familiar, warm, and comforting, like home.

It had to be Bawo. She had heard his voice. She would know that voice anywhere. And the hand that splayed possessively across her tummy. That hand belonged to Bawo. But what was he doing here? Why was he in her room? She let herself enjoy the warmth of his embrace for a few seconds, then tried to pull away.

"Amenze, don't go. We need to talk. Please hear me out."

"I am not going anywhere. Where could I possibly go? This is my room. I am just trying to sit up."

"Oh." He instantly released her.

Amenze sat and propped herself up against the headboard. While she adjusted herself, Bawo rose from the bed and moved to sit on the armchair beside the bed. He looked handsome in a purple *Kemeje*, purple and black patterned

George wrapper, and black Stetson. It was her first time seeing him dressed in Itsekiri traditional attire. She had to admit that he looked regal.

"What are you doing here?" Amenze belatedly realised that he was in her home. "How are you in my home? How did you know where I lived?"

"I arrived in Warri this morning. I wanted to see you because I was unhappy about our last encounter. Efua informed me you were in Benin."

"You didn't have to travel to Benin to see me. You could have asked Efua for my Benin number and called me."

"Some things are better discussed in person. After my trip to Warri, I had to see you. I went to Prince Jimi's home and learnt you'd left. So, I came here."

She frowned. "How did you discover I was at Prince Jimi's and find my house?"

"Mene and Bulwark guards. I am unsure how they know, but after I mentioned your name to Mene and expressed my need to see you, the Bulwark guards always seemed to know where you were.

"Mene?" Amenze furrowed her brows. He couldn't be talking about—

"Chief Mene Omajaemite. Ologbotsere of Warri Kingdom."

"Ah. That's who I thought you might refer to. Wow! You're no longer regular Warri people if the traditional prime minister accompanies you. I saw your photo on television."

Bawo looked away, taking off his Stetson and scratching his head. "About that, it's not how I intended you to find out. And I will talk about that soon. But I need to know something first."

Amenze held her breath, confident she knew what was coming next.

"What were you doing in Prince Jimi's house? Also, what is this about a prophecy?"

"Efua told you, right?"

"Yes, she did. She also told me a lot more, like how you shared pictures with her while we were in Paris and how she contacted Dimitris. She also sold the story to the press—"

"Press?!" Amenze gasped and covered her mouth with her hands. "What press?"

"Nothing that you should worry about. The same gutter press published the rumour about me months ago. She didn't do it for the money, though—it was to satisfy some personal vendetta against me. She tried to make a move on me the third time. You need to be more circumspect when choosing your friends, Amenze."

Amenze nodded in silent agreement. Trusting Efua with her private life had been a foolish mistake. She still needed to know Bawo's purpose here, but she wouldn't find out without first telling him about the prophecy and being in Prince Jimi's house.

"I was in Benin for a friend's wedding a couple of months ago. Her husband is the Chief Priest of the Benin Kingdom, and he prophesied I was the Olori of the Warri Kingdom. I thought I was going to marry the old king, and I decided to give my virginity to Dimitris, but on my return to the UK, things had changed, and his sister warned me off him.

"Then, you reappeared in my life and swept me off my feet. I was attracted to you and didn't think twice about sleeping with you. After our disagreement and the old king's death, it seemed wise to pursue the prophecy. That's why I was in Prince Jimi's home. Will you now tell me what's going on?"

"As you probably already know, I am Prince Dere Tunoka."

"Tunoka," Amenze repeated. "Warri royal family."

Bawo nodded. "That's correct. My father was born Prince Eyimofe Tunoka. He was the twelfth Olu of Warri, Olu Erejuwa I."

"You never mentioned him."

"It was not deliberate. I was not trying to deceive you. I never really accepted my paternity until recently. My mother was a palace maid many years ago. She was gorgeous. You saw a photo of her when you were at my house in Chelsea. The Portuguese had intermarried with her family, and she had Portuguese ancestry, which showed up in her genes. Her skin tone was very light, and she had waist-long hair. It wasn't long before she caught the attention of the Olu of Warri. They had an affair, and she became pregnant. The wife of the Olu was jealous, and she poisoned my mother. My aunt believed what had been given to my mother was intended to cause her to miscarry, but my mother instead went into labour.

"She was scared for her life and what would become of me, so she travelled to Ode Itsekiri, where her older sister lived. They were the only two children of their parents. Others were half-siblings. Born years apart, they were like mother and daughter, as my aunt had no child. My mother went to her to give birth to me and died shortly after."

Amenze remained silent while Bawo paused the story, stood up, and walked around the room. His face was expressionless, but she could tell that recounting the story of his birth, which was intertwined with his mother's suffering and death, was difficult.

"With my mother dead, it fell to my aunt to raise me. Once she had gone through my mother's things, she found diaries and letters–things that revealed my paternity and my name, the name my father had given me. My aunt took me before my first birthday to present me to my father, but I looked like my mother and nothing like him, so he denied that I was his child. He probably thought she was trying to deceive him. She took me again at eight years old, and once more, he denied I was his child. My aunt died after my sixteenth birthday, and having no close family to support me, I turned to my father for help. He ordered a palace guard to strip me and give me twenty-four lashes of the whip."

Amenze gasped. "No, he didn't!"

"Yes. He did! That was the last time I saw him. I was returning home to Ode Itsekiri when I met two men, a Portuguese and a Greek. The Greek man was Aristotle Papadopoulos, the father of Dimitris. The other man was Agostinho Domingo. They were great friends and in Warri because Agostinho was trying to trace the Domingo family in Ode Itsekiri. Meeting with them changed the course of my life.

Agostinho became interested in me because of the Domingo name and the certainty that we shared a common ancestry.

"I remained with them during their trip, acting as a tour guide and serving them. When it was time to return to Europe, they took me. Agostinho became my first father figure, and I lived with him in Portugal and Greece until his death when I was eighteen. At that point, Aristotle became a father figure and mentor. I owe him everything that I am today."

Amenze rested her chin on her hand as she absorbed the information. "I knew you were a protégé of Dimitris' father. I never realised the relationship was so close."

"Don't be fooled," he said. "Dimitris and I were never close. He resented his father's involvement in my life and saw me as someone competing with him for his father's love and attention. We were never friends. There was always rivalry going on. At best, he tolerated me."

"This is quite a story. So, if your father was the twelfth Olu of Warri and Prince Jimi's father was the thirteenth Olu of Warri, which one of you will be the fourteenth Olu of Warri?"

Bawo shrugged. "The throne shouldn't have gone to my uncle. I will be king."

"I see." Amenze wrapped her arms around herself to keep from trembling.

"Do you?" He reached out and pulled her to her feet and into his arms. "We could get married. You could become Olori according to the prophecy."

"You mean make the prophecy happen?"

Bawo nodded. "If you put it that way. Does it matter, though? That's what you were trying to do at Prince Jimi's house. Make the prophecy happen." He sounded jealous.

"Yeah. I guess." She pulled away from him and sat on the edge of the bed. "It's getting late. You should probably leave."

He returned to the chair and sat on the edge, leaning forward to clasp her hands in his.

"I didn't come here tonight to discuss Dimitris, Prince Jimi, or the throne. I came to talk about us."

"Us?"

"Yes. I had a lot to say, so I looked for you in London."

Amenze nodded, permitting him to carry on.

"I went to see you because I owed you an apology. I said some things I shouldn't have, and I am sorry. The thought of marriage worries me. Growing up, my aunt emphasised that a man should only take a woman's virginity if he were ready to marry her or already married to her. When I met you again, I was initially going to be your friend. I thought it would be a great way to be with you after Dimitris ended your relationship. When he did, I wanted you crying on my shoulder. Then, the night you were in my home, I realised I couldn't carry on as we were. I wanted more. But I wanted the Dimitris issue sorted out, so I asked you to break up with him."

He placed a finger over her lips as Amenze opened her mouth to speak. "I don't need you to justify why you didn't. It's not important anymore. When you came to Paris, you had already chosen me over Dimitris, even if you hadn't informed him. That night, I was looking for an easy way out. I had taken your virginity, and if I was the man Sisi Alero raised me to be, I knew I should be seriously considering marriage. I wasn't ready, so I jumped at the first sign of wrongdoing on your part and bolted."

Amenze closed her mouth, and he continued, "I seem always to say and do the wrong things where you're concerned. When Dimitris brought you to my dinner party over a year ago, I couldn't take my eyes off you. I'm unsure why because you were far removed from the women I usually dated. But I wanted you, and when he told me you were a star-struck fan, I assumed you'd jump into my bed. For years, women fell over themselves to be in my bed. Why not? I was Bawo Domingo— handsome, rich, big spender and women loved me. You can imagine my surprise when you turned me down.

"At first, I thought you were playing some silly hard-to-get game, but you told me off and asked Dimitris to take you home. I acted like I didn't care but hardly slept that night. You occupied my thoughts completely. I wanted to see you again, so the next day, I called Dimitris and told him I needed his help to contact you. I mentioned that I could not stop thinking about you and hoped you'd accept my apology and give me another chance. He laughed and asked me to stay away from you as you were his. He said he'd been meaning to ask you to date him, and he'd finally worked up the nerve to do it when taking you home that night, and you'd agreed."

"He said *what?*" Amenze couldn't believe her ears. "But that's not correct. He didn't ask me to date him until about a month after that night. Before that, we were friends, and in retrospect, we should have stayed friends because, in my mind, I never removed him from the friend zone."

"I believed him as I saw no reason why he should lie. Looking back, I think my interest in you probably sparked his interest. He believed we were in constant competition. My relationship with Aristotle had consequences, with Dimitris disliking me being one. I'm just sorry that you had to be a casualty." He pulled her off the bed and onto his lap. "He must have seen that I liked you a lot."

"You did?"

"Yes. I lied to myself that I didn't, and that I had missed nothing, but I partied hard for close to a year, trying to distract the inner longing with a lot of external noise. It wasn't easy to get you out of my mind. Every contact with Dimitris made me think of you. And I partied some more. After the scandal, I retreated into my shell."

"I am sorry to hear that, and if it's any consolation, I never forgot you either."

His eyes brightened for the first time since he arrived. "Really?"

"Yes," she affirmed. "I thought you were rude, but it didn't stop me from researching your business and personal life. That's how I learned of the scandal. And the multiple women subtly suggesting they had intimate encounters with you."

"What did you think?" His eyes and voice betrayed his concern.

"I wondered what your PR team were doing. But mostly, I thought I'd like a massage from you." She grinned cheekily.

"You are such a naughty girl, Amenze," Bawo chuckled and kissed her. "But I promise to give you a massage if you come home with me tonight. Will you? Please. I have missed you."

"Where's home?"

"I have a massive waterfront house in Warri. It's as big as the palace. I built it three years ago using a construction company that House of Oma owns."

Amenze rolled her eyes. "House of Oma owns everything, doesn't it?" She got off his lap to pack an overnight bag.

Bawo shrugged. "Well, I tried to put much distance between me and poverty."

"Oh, please," Amenze scoffed. "This has gone from wanting to escape poverty to wanting world domination."

Bawo rose to his feet as she moved around the room, throwing things into a small suitcase. "Call it what you want. What would you know about poverty? You were raised in an upper-middle-class family." He looked around her nicely furnished bedroom.

"And you're Olu Erejuwa's son and heir!" she threw back at him. "Warri is oil-rich!"

"True! And while he's left me a sizeable portion of his estate, I got it when I didn't need it. I was poorer than you growing up."

"Still, your father's richer than mine!"

The banter went on as Amenze packed her bag and got dressed.

CHAPTER SIXTEEN

Bawo stood in the bathroom doorway, his arms crossed, his shoulder leaning against the door frame as he watched Amenze throw up what must be her entire breakfast. His gut feeling told him what this was. As he stared at her, he didn't feel fear. Instead, he felt something else, excitement, overtaken almost immediately by anger.

"Is this what I think it is?" he demanded. When he got no response, he rephrased the question. "Are you pregnant?"

She didn't look at him as she stood and walked to the sink to pour some cold water on her face. "My period was late, and I thought I might be. I had a test yesterday, and it was positive."

Bawo scowled. "I see. Is it mine?"

Amenze nodded. Bawo believed her. It was unlikely that a woman who remained a virgin for over a year while dating Dimitris would rapidly move on to another bed and become pregnant. But what enraged him was learning this after knowing she had been in Prince Jimi's house the evening before.

"When were you planning to inform me?" He gave her no time to answer. "No, let me guess. You weren't planning to inform me, were you? A prophecy foretold your destiny as

Olori. Instead of informing me of your pregnancy, you aimed to marry the crown prince and potentially pass off my baby as his."

Amenze was speechless with astonishment, and tears quickly welled up in her eyes, blurring her view.

"It wasn't like that, Bawo," she quietly refuted.

"*It wasn't like that?*" Bawo shouted in rage. "How was it, Amenze? Pray, enlighten me! I searched for you in London but was told you had returned home to Benin to fulfil a prophecy of becoming Olori. And when I arrived, I learnt you were wooing the crown prince. Pregnant for me but wooing him to secure a marriage proposal. Suppose he asked you to marry him, what would your response have been, *Aya mi?*"

Bawo stood with hands thrust deeply into the pants of his loungewear, watching Amenze as her tears fell. Inside his head, he willed her to say no. He willed her to say she would have rejected Prince Jimi's proposal because she was carrying his child.

"Yes," she whispered.

Bawo wondered how he remained standing outwardly while crumbling inwardly. His eyes remained fixed on her for quite a while. "Just as I feared. And you would have persuaded him to have a quick wedding and wedding night and then convinced him that the baby was his and born prematurely. Or perhaps you would have aborted my baby to secure your place as Olori."

Her eyes widened in shock, and she shook her head vehemently. "I could never have killed your baby, Bawo. I love you."

The woman had a nerve, Bawo thought angrily.

"Shut up!" he shouted at her. "It's clear that you don't love me! You do not know what love is. You are a liar and schemer, and you're only here because Erejuwa was my father. Well, your ambition, which drove you, although you were carrying my child in your womb, will now be your undoing. Prince Jimi hasn't got a prayer of becoming Olu. The throne was never his father's and won't be his. I will be Olu, but you will never be my Olori. We'll marry promptly, and you'll stay in the palace until my child is born. Then, I'll replace you with an Olori of my choice."

As Bawo turned and walked off, Amenze fell to the floor in a crumpled heap, her quiet sobs echoing through the enormous state-of-the-art bathroom. Bawo arranged for a driver to take her to Benin immediately. It seemed to Amenze that he could not wait to remove her presence from his home. She went gladly, as Bawo had transformed into an unrecognisable man, unlike the lover who had passionately made love to her the previous night and served her breakfast in bed this morning, along with a romantic marriage proposal and a white gold diamond cluster ring.

Rushing the wedding was for the best. Planning a Benin traditional marriage ceremony in nine days would keep her too busy to think of Bawo. She informed her parents of the wedding first. Her mother sang and danced while her father drilled her with questions. She had to tell them she was already confirmed pregnant. She then had to convince her father that she and Bawo were in love, and he wasn't marrying her because of the baby. Then she called her brothers in America and answered questions similar to the kind her father had thrown at her. Finally, she told her friends.

Ede, Eki and Tiyan wasted no time organising a small celebration at Eki's residence in the palace, where they took turns gushing over her diamond engagement ring. They did not mention her visit to Prince Jimi or whether anyone thought they'd made an error in judgement. Instead, they put their heads together to plan a flamboyant traditional marriage ceremony for their last unmarried friend.

In the days leading up to the wedding, Amenze didn't speak to Bawo. He sent the palace staff to her to ensure she had everything she required for the wedding. Every morning, without fail, he would text her to check in and make sure she was doing okay. But she sensed he did it out of a sense of duty because she was pregnant and hated that. She wanted to talk to him, but she couldn't. Bawo attended endless meetings with the inner caucus chiefs, and news reached her of the fights between him and Prince Jimi and those loyal to them.

She yearned to connect with the man she loved, but he had erected a barrier between them, and she sensed that talking about his quest for kingship was forbidden. Amenze couldn't help but feel a pang of sorrow instead of the expected happiness as her wedding day grew nearer.

The day of her traditional marriage ceremony arrived. The ceremony was full of fanfare and more enormous than she had expected. Her family went all out. Her brothers flew in from America with their families. Eki, Tiyan, and Ede, along with their spouses, were present, all glamorously dressed in traditional attire and ready to support her big day. Bawo arrived in the company of many palace chiefs and some friends and business partners who had flown in that morning from Europe.

Amenze tried to smile and look as joyful as they all thought she should feel, but inside, she was dying. When she was led into the large marquee erected on the extensive grounds of her parents' home and stood before Bawo, she could see that he looked just as miserable as she did. He also looked tired and strained. She longed to touch him, but she couldn't, and even when it became mandatory, she could swear he flinched just a little at her touch.

With a broken heart, she went through the motions of the ceremony. Once it was over, she was escorted in a convoy to Bawo's residence in Warri, where Bawo, who preceded her to Warri, received her at a lavish dinner party. The party, designed to be low-key as the kingdom was still officially mourning for Olu Ginuwa III, continued into the early morning hours.

Once the guests dispersed, Amenze was left alone. Bawo did not bother to spend their wedding night with her. He slept in the master bedroom suite, leaving her alone in the mistress bedroom suite, which was the designated bridal suite. She wept through the night and fell asleep at the first signs of daylight.

*****

Bawo rose from bed long before the crack of dawn and made his way downstairs to the fully equipped gym. A one-hour run on the treadmill was what he needed to clear his head. He had not been sleeping well. Having Amenze sleeping under his roof as his wife and not being able to touch her was becoming a little too much for him to handle. How could he touch her when he believed she was only with him because he would be king? He served only as a means to an end, to help her achieve her ambition of being queen.

As he sprinted on the treadmill, he considered the question he had asked for many days. Would she have agreed to marry him if he had shown up in her home as just Bawo Domingo without being Erejuwa's son? He was certain she would have rejected him and kept plotting to win Prince Jimi. Even now, the gods forbid, if Prince Jimi were chosen as Olu Designate, would Amenze happily remain with him? Would she end their marriage and pursue Prince Jimi? His fear of being rejected or tolerated by her was real.

He could not think about that now. He had a big day ahead of him. Today, the Olu Designate would be declared. The battle had not been easy. If he assumed he would walk into the palace, announce that he was Erejuwa's only son and heir, and then be handed the throne, he was quickly disabused of that notion.

Prince Jimi was fighting with everything he had to sit on the throne his father had just vacated. His mother, Olori Ginuwa III, was fiercely behind her son. Even more disturbing was that the wife of Olu Erejuwa I, Olori Erejuwa I, was also backing Prince Jimi's bid to become king. Not that Olori Erejuwa I particularly cared for Olori Ginuwa III or Prince Jimi, but Bawo was a common enemy, and both women united over this. Bawo knew they had bribed many of the chiefs. A significant reason the battle had been drawn out.

They had debated the same issue since his arrival in Warri a little over two weeks ago. His identity. Those loyal to Olu Ginuwa III had initially put forth powerful reasons he should not be king. They had claimed they did not know him, and his father had not openly acknowledged him. But Chief Temi Jacdonmi, who was taken into Olu Erejuwa's confidence and given specific choice properties to hold in trust for him, had come forward to say that it was not true and had evidence to show that Olu Erejuwa I had acknowledged Prince Dere as his son.

Then, they claimed there was a possibility that Bawo was an impostor and not Prince Dere, Olu Erejuwa's son. But Mene had produced evidence of the DNA test, and Bawo had put forward his mother's diaries and the letters exchanged between his parents.

Despite the evidence, the debate continued, and each time he appeared in the palace for a meeting, some chief needed to be convinced of his identity. It had been exhausting. Ultimately, the chiefs had no say; only Ife did; hence, the oracle was consulted. Today, Chief Ayo Esigbone, the mouthpiece of the gods and the Chief Priest of the Warri Kingdom, would attend the meeting and pronounce the Olu Designate as ordained by the gods.

Feeling energised after his run, Bawo showered and dressed carefully in a black George wrapper and *Kemeje*. He tied his wrapper so the pleats gathered to one side of his waist, and the excess cloth slid to the ground in a long trail behind him. On his neck and wrists, he wore red coral beads belonging to his late father; on his head, a black Stetson with a decorative feather. He completed his attire with a sleek pair of black Italian designer shoes and was all set to go.

Amenze was still in bed, and he didn't have to endure any awkwardness over breakfast. But as he ate, he couldn't keep his eyes from straying to the other end of the ten-seater dining table. The few times they had eaten together since their wedding, she had sat there, putting distance between them. If his housekeeper, Mrs Uku, or any of the housemaids found it strange, they said nothing, and their body language revealed nothing. As with all his domestic staff, where they existed, they were discreet. Emami's primary goal was discretion when employing anyone to work closely with Bawo.

As he was chauffeur driven to the palace for his meetings in the 1963 Rolls Royce Silver Cloud, which he had recently inherited from his late father, he pushed thoughts of his beautiful wife out of his mind and focused on the day ahead.

Mene was already at the palace, waiting for him when he arrived. That didn't surprise him much, as it had been the usual practice. What did, however, was being informed that he had an impromptu meeting with his father's wife, Olori Erejuwa I, and her daughters, his half-sisters, Princess Roli Tunoka and Princess Tsemaye Tunoka. They were the oldest of Olu Erejuwa's children and the only two born in his marriage.

He was taken aback. *What had brought this on?* He wondered.

"Your sisters are naturally curious, albeit a little wary," Mene informed him. "As for Olori Erejuwa I, her motives are unclear."

This wasn't good and would dampen his mood before the charged meeting with Prince Jimi and his supporters. He walked down the main hallway with Mene, ignoring the photographs of his ancestors on the walls and the royal insignia of Olu Ginuwa III crested on the luxurious red carpet. Mene stopped and opened a door at the end of the hall. Bawo was then ushered into a beautiful, well-lighted meeting room with plush ornate furnishing. Inside, three women wearing traditional Itsekiri attire of two wrappers, blouses, and gele head ties awaited him. Both sisters were older than him by possibly three to five years.

Mene duly performed the introductions, and Princess Tsemaye Tunoka, who looked like the younger sister, approached him, taking his hands in hers.

"It is so good to meet you finally. It's almost like seeing a ghost," she said. "You walk exactly as he did. Your body language is so similar."

He was unsure how to respond, but a response was not immediately required as Olori Erejuwa I had risen to her feet and stared at him, as one might stare at the dirt on the bottom of their costly shoes.

"So, you are the bastard born by a maid who thinks he can be king?"

There was a gasp from both princesses. Tsemaye put a hand over her mouth while Roli shifted uncomfortably in her seat and avoided looking at Bawo.

"My Olori, there are no bastards in Itsekiri land. You know this. Prince Dere has the same rights as your daughters." Mene recovered quickly enough to correct the widowed queen.

Bawo stared at the woman before him, wondering why she requested to see him. This was the woman who poisoned his mother and caused her death. And after all these years, knowing she killed his mother, she was still filled with so much hate?

"Is that why you asked to see me? To inform me I am a bastard?"

"You are as ambitious as your mother, trying to rise above your station in life!" She raised her voice. "The maid wanted to be queen. As if giving the king a male child was all that qualified a nobody like her to be queen. Well, she never became Olori, and you will never be Olu.

"I want you to know that I will contest whatever properties my husband left you. I don't know what games you and Chief Temi Jacdonmi are playing, but you have no right to those properties. No right at all. You also have no right to the throne. You will never sit on it."

Mene was about to respond, but Bawo raised a hand to stop him. This was his battle, and he could fight it without Mene's help.

"I have a letter from my father saying that his throne is mine and it will be mine. I couldn't be bothered with it for thirty-three years, but now that I am bothered enough to leave my little kingdom in Europe to seek my father's throne, I will sit on it. Not you, Prince Jimi, his mother and sisters, or the chiefs you have bribed will stop it. My name is Onetoritsebawoete. The one whom God backs does not fail.

"I have never failed, and I won't be failing today. When I leave this palace later today, I will leave as Olu Designate, and in ninety days, I will be crowned Olu in Ode Itsekiri, the land of my birth. And when I become king, you and the wife of Olu

Ginuwa III will be stripped of your Olori titles. You will both revert to being addressed as Princess Tunoka. Only my wife shall be the Olori in this kingdom."

He turned to leave the room, satisfied that Olori Erejuwa I was now speechless from shock. He paused as he reached the door and turned to look at all three women, his eyes hardening as they set on his father's wife.

"I could banish you from Itsekiri land altogether, especially after what you did to my mother, but what would that serve?"

Princess Roli hurried after him as he walked away and called, "Dere, wait!"

He stopped and turned to face her—his father's oldest child. She had Erejuwa's face—the face Bawo was punished for not having.

She took his hands as Tsemaye had done earlier. "I am sorry. Her comment to you was uncalled for—and Tsemaye's right. You have our father's personality. It is like looking at a ghost."

Bawo laughed then and embraced her. Surprisingly, Tsemaye approached and squeezed in, and it became a group hug. He vowed to get acquainted with all his half-sisters. While he was glad to have met his older sisters, the meeting with Olori

Erejuwa I had left an unpleasant taste in his mouth, so he was on a short fuse as he began the meeting with the palace chiefs that morning.

His temper grew as the debate of who would be a better king continued and became more heated, with chiefs shamelessly resorting to name-calling. Tiring of the chaos, he rose and shouted at everyone, young and elderly chiefs alike.

"Silence!" He had had enough. "Not another word from any of you! This meeting will adjourn until the chief priest joins us and declares who the Olu Designate is."

The room became instantly quiet. So quiet a pin dropping to the floor would not have gone unnoticed.

"For a moment, I forgot Olu Erejuwa I had joined his ancestors. You sounded just like him," Chief Noyo Sagay, who was unapologetically loyal to Olu Ginuwa III, grudgingly admitted.

Everyone instantly agreed. It was the first time the entire cabinet of chiefs spoke with one voice and declared that Bawo was Olu Erejuwa's son. It was his first display of rage, and although he had not planned to lose his temper, he admitted it had brought him a small win.

A break ensued to allow people to calm down, refresh themselves, meet in smaller groups, and ultimately await the chief priest. It was several hours before he arrived. Without a traditional long-sleeved shirt covering his chest and no shoes on his feet, he entered the main meeting room wearing only a white George wrapper around his waist and white coral beads around his neck, wrists, and ankles. Standing in the centre of the room, he appeared formidable.

Bawo and Prince Jimi rose and approached him. Behind them, the chiefs gathered, everyone waiting with bated breath for *Okparan-umale* to speak. He ignored Prince Jimi and gave his full attention to Bawo.

"The gods of our land welcome you home, *Omoba*. Our king and our pride." With those words, he delivered the verdict. Bawo was Olu Designate.

Joy erupted in the camp of those loyal to Bawo and his father. Chief Mene Omajaemite and Chief Temi Jacdonmi stood on either side of Bawo, each man raising one of his hands while the others chanted, "*Omoba!*"

The sound of joy and rejoicing was so loud that no one noticed Prince Jimi and his cronies exiting. Not that he had many cronies left. Many in his camp instantly switched sides, pitching their tent with the in-coming Olu of Warri Kingdom.

Congratulatory messages poured in from outside the Warri Kingdom. The Oba of Benin and the other royal fathers who had pledged their support to Bawo and followed the drama closely called one after the other. Bawo heartily received their well wishes, but his greatest desire was to return to Amenze and tell her the good news.

As he travelled home in the back seat of the classic Rolls Royce, which now bore the customised registration plate, Olu Designate, Bawo thought about his beautiful wife and their very young marriage, which had not begun well. With the realisation that she was his wife and would eventually become his queen, Bawo concluded it was time to mend the rift. She'd made an error of judgement and aroused his jealousy. She had roused more than his jealousy. Her actions had roused the deep-seated fear of rejection he had struggled with as a child and young adult after being continually rejected by his father.

However, he'd had ample time to contemplate the matter calmly. He was compelled to consider the matter rationally. Amenze's father and brothers were protective of her. They could storm his home and take her away if they suspected she was unhappy.

His private meeting with them on the day of his and Amenze's traditional wedding ceremony had been brief but memorable. They'd looked unfriendly as they informed him they did not think Amenze should marry him just because she was pregnant. Her oldest brother, Norense, had announced that he was calling off the wedding because he suspected

Amenze was being pressured to go ahead with it because she was pregnant.

Bawo had sounded like a used car salesman as he desperately tried to convince all four men that he cared very much for Amenze and would make her happy. But he had not done that. He knew she was unhappy.

He sighed as a heavy cloud of sadness engulfed him. And what for? So, she had gone to Prince Jimi's house to fulfil a prophecy, and she had done so knowing she was pregnant with his child. She had admitted she would have accepted Prince Jimi's marriage proposal. But Prince Jimi hadn't proposed. He didn't have a clue why Amenze had been in his home.

Bawo had asked around and learnt that Amenze had discussed Elevate with Prince Jimi. And if she had felt she needed to pursue a prophecy instead of telling him about her pregnancy, who was to blame for that? He had called her manipulative and said he would not marry her. What was she supposed to do after that?

Bawo groaned and rubbed his temple. Yes. It was time to release past grievances. He was now king. The last of his fears had been eliminated. Amenze wasn't going anywhere.

CHAPTER SEVENTEEN

Amenze knew the decision on who would become Olu Designate would be made that day. Bawo departed from home early that morning, even before she woke up. Her day was occupied with conference calls with Eki, Tiyan, and the London office staff. They deliberated on lessons learned from the previous pitch event and selected a new date and venue for the next one.

She had dinner alone and retired to bed with a novel she planned to read until she fell asleep. However, she could not focus. Thoughts of Bawo and his quest for kingship occupied her thoughts. She earnestly advocated for his selection as Olu Designate. Bawo was a good man who deserved his birthright. She did not doubt that he would make an exceptional king.

The battle was intense, and it saddened her that he fought without her by his side. She laughed without mirth. Why would Bawo require her support after she admitted she would have agreed to marry Prince Jimi while expecting their child? It was a marvel he married her at all. If any of her brothers' wives had conducted themselves like that before tying the knot, she would have advised her brother to reconsider.

The state of her relationship with Bawo was beyond belief, all because of a foolish prophecy. A prophecy she should have left well alone and not tried to fulfil. Usi had warned her, but she hadn't listened. If she had done nothing, absolutely nothing, Bawo would have got over his initial displeasure and come looking for her, and they would be here now, working together towards his bid to become king. Love and laughter would fill their home. However, because she had attempted to fulfil the prophecy, she and Bawo stopped talking, and sadness filled their home.

In pursuing Prince Jimi, she hurt the man she loved and made it worse by stating she would have married Prince Jimi had he asked her. What had possessed her to say that when it wasn't entirely true? If Prince Jimi had proposed, she would have told him she was pregnant and waited for his reaction. She would only have said yes if Prince Jimi, knowing she was pregnant by another man, was still willing to marry her. And she would only have proceeded with Prince Jimi believing that Bawo didn't want her.

Bawo believed she was so determined to be Olori that she would have killed his baby or passed it off as Prince Jimi's. She couldn't blame him. Her actions made her look ambitious and desperate. How did she get to that point? She received a prophecy that she would be queen, but it wasn't something she wanted. She only hoped to find love, get married, and start a family. Her husband didn't need to be a king.

However, she had received a prophecy and relentlessly pursued it to her downfall. The prophecy was slipping away as Bawo refused to make her Olori. However, she wasn't bothered by that. She didn't want to be Olori. All she wanted was to be Bawo's wife. Bawo's only wife. For the rest of her life. Yet, her quest to become Olori prevented her from obtaining even that.

Bawo had said that once the baby was born, he would divorce her and marry one who would be Olori. The mere thought of another woman becoming Bawo's wife, sharing his bed, and carrying his child in her womb was sufficient to send her to a mental asylum, where she would not recover but expire.

It was midnight when she heard car doors slamming, suggesting that Bawo had returned home. Had he got it? Was he the Olu Designate? Exhausted from attempting to read, she set aside her book, lay down, and closed her eyes. If he were Olu Designate, she would hear about it from the housekeeper or maids in the morning.

As Amenze drifted into sleep, she suddenly felt a subtle indentation in the mattress beneath her. Her eyes fluttered open. Bawo sat cross-legged at the end of her bed, dressed in his pyjamas. Finding him in her bedroom was unexpected, and even more surprising was his lack of anger. He had a smile on his face.

"Is it over?" She sat up slowly. "Did you get it?"

"*We* got it, *Aya mi.*" He took her hand and lifted it to his lips. "My queen."

"Oh, Bawo!" Amenze struggled to hold back the tears as she threw herself into his arms. "This is the best news I've heard in a long time."

She pulled back and stroked his face, all her love for him shining through her eyes. "Bawo, you deserve this throne. You will be an excellent king. You were born for this. Your parents would be so pleased and so proud."

His eyes shone with unshed tears as he nodded. "I think so too. And my aunt, Sisi Alero. She never stopped believing that I would be king."

"She was an exceptional woman. She did a brilliant job preparing you," Amenze said. "I think we should go to Ode Itsekiri. Your mother and aunt are buried there. Your father, too. You could visit them."

"You'll come with me?"

"I am your wife, Bawo." Amenze placed her hands in his. "I'll go with you anywhere you want me to."

"Amenze, about—"

Amenze put her hand over his lips to silence him even as she gently shook her head. "I do not fault your decision, Bawo, and I accept it. Not being queen doesn't trouble me. I am honoured and content to be your wife. And for the time that you allow me to have that honour, I will support you as best as I can."

"That's not what I want, *Aya mi*. I want more. I'm not happy," Bawo blurted out. "Today, a wrong done to me for thirty-three years was corrected. Today, my birthright was restored to me, and I should be overjoyed, but I am not. My heart yearns for you. The distance between us is maddening. I miss you, and it's so lonely without you. Please come back. I long for the companionship, the banter, and the laughter."

Amenze stared in silence, and the tears slowly gathered. She opened her mouth, but no words followed.

Bawo grasped her hands. "*Aya mi*, I'm sorry. I love you. I will be better. I promise. Please say something."

"I don't know what to say." Amenze's voice was a whisper, and the tears blurred her view.

Bawo gently brushed away a tear as it fell. "Do you love me?"

"I love you, Bawo. I love you very much."

"Then let's start again," he urged. "As man and wife, as king and queen."

"Bawo, I'm scared."

"What's scaring you?" he asked. "Tell me, I'll fix it."

"It's been a roller-coaster ride. One moment, we're happy, and the next, I do something wrong, and you reject me. I can't bear it happening again."

"*Aya mi*, I promise you, whatever the future brings, we will deal with it as a couple. This is the longest I have been with a woman. I am learning; we're both learning. You are right. It's been a roller-coaster ride; I know I haven't handled our misunderstandings properly. I am a jealous man, and like you, I am afraid of rejection."

Amenze sat quietly, studying him when he was done. It was ironic that she feared his rejection while he feared hers.

"I am sorry, Bawo, I didn't see it in this light, honestly." She chewed on her bottom lip. "But I promise you, I don't love Prince Jimi or desire him. I only went for that meeting because I believed you didn't want me and that Prince Jimi was the one I was prophesied to marry. When I found out I was pregnant, the appointment to see him had been made, and in hindsight, I should never have proceeded with the meeting."

"But you were curious?"

Amenze nodded. "I was, but I promise you, Bawo, I would never have killed your baby or tricked Prince Jimi into thinking it was his. I need you to believe this."

"If I didn't believe it, *Aya mi*, I would never have married you. I believed it. I was angry and hurt that you would have accepted Prince Jimi's marriage proposal." He grimaced. "But there wasn't any, so I don't want to discuss the issue further. Let's put the unpleasant past behind us and move forward."

Amenze tenderly held his face in her hands. "Anything you want, Bawo. I'm that much in love with you."

"I told you that night in my home in Chelsea that you belonged in a palace, and now I get to take you there." He leaned in and pressed his lips to hers in a fleeting, passionate kiss.

Amenze locked eyes with Bawo as the kiss ended; a silent intensity passed between them. "Are you certain about wanting me as Olori?"

Bawo groaned and gathered her into his arms so she could sit on his lap. "The things I said that morning, I didn't mean them. It was my jealousy and insecurity talking, *Aya mi*. I could never choose another. You are everything that I want. I love you. I think I have loved you from the moment Dimitris brought you to my Mayfair apartment."

"I love you too," Amenze murmured as she wrapped her arms around his neck and touched her lips to his.

"I love you more," he whispered against her mouth.

With an arm wrapped around her and the other cradling the back of her head, Bawo angled his head to deepen the kiss. As the kiss lingered, it became intensified and more urgent, and Amenze pulled away. He appeared puzzled while she removed her black silk nightgown and discarded it on the floor.

As she settled back onto the pillows, she raised a brow. "Well, are you going to stare all night, Ogiame?"

He grinned as he took off his pyjama top and tossed it on the floor beside her nightgown.

"Challenge accepted, *Aya mi*. Show me what you've got." His mouth came down, crushing hers, even as his body covered hers.

*****

Amenze woke to the feel of Bawo's large hands gently massaging her back. It was pure bliss. She could get used to this. She smiled as she cast her mind back to the last ninety days.

The day after Bawo was elected Olu Designate, she went with him to visit the graves of his father, mother, and aunt in Ode Itsekiri. He ordered new gravestones for them, the one for his mother showing her status as the king's mother.

She had not expected a honeymoon as she knew Bawo was supposed to be in *Idaniken*, a time of seclusion and preparation for ninety days as he awaited his coronation. Still, he had quietly whisked her off to Europe for five nights. They spent two nights onboard his yacht, Oma, sailing on the Mediterranean, and on the second night, he had taken her to dinner in Monaco.

On their return trip, they made a brief stop in London, as Bawo had arranged for them to get married in a registry office ceremony. His friend Suf and his private secretary, Emami, were their witnesses. Bawo told her he'd intended it to disabuse her of any thought he might take another wife.

The trip and the second wedding were pleasant surprises, and by the time they returned to Warri, she was more in love with her husband than before their traditional Benin marriage rites.

Once they returned, arrangements began earnestly for Olu Ginuwa III's traditional funeral rites. As Olu Designate, Bawo performed specific traditional rites to send forth his predecessor. After the burial rites, the kingdom shifted its focus to the Olu Designate and the preparations for his coronation. Now, the day that the entire kingdom had eagerly awaited had finally come.

"Turn over," Bawo whispered, snapping her out of her daydream.

Half asleep, Amenze obeyed, and Bawo splayed his hands over her tiny baby bump. He kissed the bump and then kissed her. "I need to go now."

Amenze knew this. It was time for him to prepare for the busy day ahead. The *Agbuda* would soon arrive to assist the Olu Designate in donning his traditional attire for the ceremony. She had maids on their way to help her dress, so she was willing to release him. Yet, she couldn't resist pulling him back for one more passionate kiss.

"Good morning, Ogiame."

"Save that for later tonight, *Aya mi*. When I am officially Ogiame," he said jokingly.

"I most certainly will," she assured him.

She lay on her side and watched as he dressed in his pyjamas. "Go straight to your bedroom, and do not stop at the harem."

There was no harem. Bawo had clarified that he intended to have only one wife. But Amenze loved to tease him about it.

"If there were a harem, the concubines would have left in anger, given how you've selfishly and unreasonably chained me to your bed the past ninety days. Literally." He got on the bed and spanked her backside as he spoke, then scuttled off the bed before she could retaliate.

But a giggling Amenze playfully tossed a pillow after him as he hurried towards the door. It narrowly missed him, and he turned to her with a mock scowl.

"You're a fortunate woman, *Aya mi*; imagine what the Itsekiri people would say if I showed up for my coronation with a black eye."

Then he was gone, leaving Amenze rolling her eyes in mock exasperation and chuckling softly.

EPILOGUE

The Coronation Ceremony....

In contemplative silence, Bawo stepped onto the large boat that would take him through a colourful regatta to Ode Itsekiri, where he would be crowned king. He was dressed in a white silk George wrapper paired with a red *Kemeje* and red shoes, and he exchanged his Stetson hat for a feathered red headband.

The chiefs of the Warri Kingdom were on his boat, wearing white *Kemejes,* wrappers and red double satin sashes. Twenty-four boat paddlers, twelve on each side, were dressed in red knee-length shorts, sleeveless shirts, and berets. Their outfits blended well with the red fabrics decorating the boat. Resting on the red roof of the boat was a replica of the crown. Chiefs with their *Udas* stood in front and behind the boat, singing and dancing.

The king's boat took the lead, with a fleet of boats following closely behind in the regatta. A few boats carried individuals from the royal household. One was explicitly designated for Amenze and her maids. Boats transported influential Itsekiri individuals who had come from distant places to attend the coronation ceremony.

Various boats transported kings, queens, and royal dignitaries visiting from across Africa and beyond. Each community in the kingdom had a boat. Like the king's boat, they all had a colour theme that dictated the colour of the decorative fabrics and paddlers' uniforms. All the boats had drummers and singers, and *Omoko* dancers were positioned in front and behind.

The procession slowly approached Ode Itsekiri while the singers sang the praises of the soon-to-be king and the Itsekiri people. The drummers beat their drums in tune to the singing, and the *Omoko* dancers, decked in colourful gele head ties strung together around their waists, with hand fans in their hands, performed many acrobatic displays in rhythm to the drumbeat and singing. With each jump and twirl, the head ties unfurled and spun, creating a breathtaking array of colours.

Journalists and videographers in helicopters flew above the procession to capture an aerial view of the vibrant boat regatta. After about an hour, they reached the shores of Ode Itsekiri, where the entire town had come out gorgeously dressed in traditional attires with singers and dancers to await the man who would soon be their king.

As Bawo climbed out of the boat and stood on the riverbank, he watched the scene before him. The shore and streets were overflowing with people for the coronation ceremony. These individuals had gathered solely because of him. There was no denying the transformation in his life. He was born and raised in this town. Although he had not resembled a prince, he was about to become king.

Tradition required him to fulfil certain rites, so as others made their way to the town hall, he went with his chiefs toward the palace, smiling and waving to the crowds that lined the streets.

At the palace, he received a briefing from Chief Temi Jacdonmi. The three symbolic rites he was supposed to perform were acts of labour. He had performed similar tasks growing up in Ode Itsekiri. Completing them before the coronation indicated that he was performing them for the last time. The Itsekiri people regarded their king as divine; hence, he refrained from menial tasks like fetching water, chopping wood, or paddling a canoe.

He commenced the water-fetching ritual and was observed with great curiosity by the chiefs, the crowd, and the pressmen who followed them to the palace. After fetching water, he raised the empty clay pot with both hands, rotated it around his head three times, and forcefully shattered it onto the ground.

Never again, he thought.

An axe was given to him, and he effortlessly chopped a log of wood. Upon completion, he held the axe in his right hand, spun it around his head three times, and then hurled it as far as he could.

Never again, he told himself.

Eventually, he boarded a motionless canoe accompanied by a few chiefs. After several minutes of paddling, he climbed out and twirled the paddle around his head three times before throwing it away. The chiefs praised him, and jubilation spread through the crowd.

He was led to the next ritual, which involved choosing a sword. Before him lay the swords of his thirteen predecessors. A king's name was inscribed on every sword, and there was a sword without a name. The expectation was for him to choose one and assume that king's name as his ruling name until he joined his ancestors. Choosing the nameless sword gave him the opportunity to select his own ruling name.

He was blindfolded for this ritual. As the blindfold covered his eyes, he closed them shut. For the past ninety days, he had been anxious about this moment. Imagine if he chose the sword of an infamous king and had to rule under his name forever. However, his level-headed wife told him to relax when he expressed his worries.

"You will pick the sword that you are meant to pick. It is already predestined, like your being Olu Designate."

He drew strength from her words as he leaned over the pedestal holding the swords. He touched the first three on each side, but none felt right. While moving towards the centre, his hand brushed against a sword's hilt, prompting him to pick it up without hesitation. He removed the blindfold and realised he had chosen his late father's sword. He would be crowned Olu Erejuwa II.

As he turned to look toward the chiefs, Mene smiled at him approvingly. It was as it should be. With the rituals now completed, the *Agbuda* led him inside the palace and helped him change his attire.

An hour later, Bawo was dressed in a white and gold patterned silk George wrapper, a white *Kemeje,* and a red floor-length cape with gold trimmings. He wore his father's coral beads on his neck and wrists and a white wide-brimmed Stetson on his head. He was ready for the lengthy trek to the town hall.

The crowd outside the gates cheered as he emerged from the palace. As the praise singers sang the Itsekiri national anthem, a serene and beautiful song, silence fell, and everyone remained still.

Ara o lori re, Olo rire Afo ma sin Olu R' omi.

(I hail the generous one, the unchallenged ruler (king) of water)

Owa mi (ene) ogie.

(Oh, my father)

Ira wo gba gba mi je, Mo ri guara guowun.

(When you gave me food to eat, I was very robust)

Ira wee gba gba mi je Mo ri gbe ji were.

(When you ceased to give me food to eat, I became very skinny)

Eh! Ara O lori re, O lori re Afo ma sin Olu R' omi.

(I hail the generous one, the unchallenged ruler (king) of water)

Owa mi (ene) ogie.

(Oh, my father)

Ogiame suooo!

(Your Majesty! Long may you reign!)

The parade progressed toward the heart of the town. The praise singers led the way, followed by the drummers and dancers. Following them were the palace servants adorned in white *Kemejes* and wrappers. Two red sashes, starting from the shoulder and ending at the waist, passed in opposite directions, forming a criss-cross pattern across their chests and backs.

The servants bore the throne and the crown. Positioned behind them were two servants carrying the *Uda* and *Eben* royal sceptres. Majestically, Bawo walked behind them, with the chiefs of the Warri Kingdom in his wake. On either side, the procession was flanked by palace guards working tirelessly with Bulwark guards to control the crowds.

The throne was already set in its place when he arrived at the hall filled with over five thousand guests. The servants bearing the *Uda* and *Eben* royal sceptres stood behind the throne. Amenze had already assumed her place on her throne, a smaller, more feminine version of his situated next to his. Her outfit comprised a silver sequined embellished blouse, two white embroidered lace George wrappers, and a white gele head tie, making her look radiant.

Bawo removed his Stetson, gave it to an *Agbuda* member, and walked into the hall. Everyone stood up as he approached the grand golden throne, inscribed with his name, Prince Dere Tunoka and his royal insignia. He took a moment to observe his surroundings.

The front row included important figures such as the Oba of Benin, the Obi of Agbor, the Oba of Lagos, the King of the Niger Delta, and other royal fathers. He spotted Suf and Emami somewhere in the second row. They had flown in on his jet that morning. He smiled to himself. They were his people; he could trust them to be in his corner, whatever life presented.

He glimpsed Amenze's parents, brothers, and spouses in the second row. His relationship with them had improved since the last time he'd seen them at his traditional wedding, especially since he'd married Amenze at the registry office ceremony in London.

His older sisters, Princess Roli Tunoka and Princess Tsemaye Tunoka, were present and in their designated spots in the front row. They had visited him while he was in *Idaniken*; all his sisters had, and he had cherished the experience. He hoped to see more of them and establish a good relationship with them during his reign. Olori Erejuwa I was unavoidably absent, as were Olori Ginuwa III and Prince Jimi Tunoka.

Everyone remained standing as he gracefully took his seat on the throne. The entire experience seemed surreal. As soon as he sat down, everyone else followed suit. Chief Mene Omajaemite and Chief Temi Jacdonmi came forward. Mene approached Bawo, holding the crown in his hands. As he reached Bawo, he stopped, turned towards the crowd, and revealed his intentions.

The air resounded with cries of "crown him" even before he finished. With steady hands, Mene lifted the crown and circled Bawo's head thrice, calling out in a loud voice *Omoba*. Then he lowered the crown, placing it firmly on Bawo's head.

Bawo felt like he was in a dream as the weight of the twenty-four-karat pure gold crown worn by his ancestors rested on his head. He glanced to the left and saw Amenze watching him with wonder. He gave her a wink, and she responded with a smile. People all around him were dropping to their knees to salute the new king, and there were cries of *Itsekiri de de! Iwere de de! Ogiame suooo!*

Chief Temi Jacdonmi promptly announced the new king's ruling title. The announcement of his new title as Ogiame Erejuwa II, the fourteenth Olu of Warri Kingdom, sparked jubilation among the people in the hall and those outside in the streets.

Amenze rose from her throne and knelt before him to pay homage. He locked eyes with hers briefly before she lowered her gaze.

"*Ogiame, suooo,*" she saluted, rose to her feet and returned to sit on her throne.

The chiefs of Warri Kingdom came forward and dropped on one knee to pay homage to their new king. Next, the prominent Itsekiri sons and daughters came forward to pay tribute, and then the royal fathers took turns paying homage to the Olu of Warri. With much pomp and circumstance, the kings and their entourages paid homage to the new king.

Next, it was the turn of the praise singers. The drummers and *Omoko* dancers joined them as they took centre stage. Once more, the Itsekiri anthem was sung, and the newly crowned king saluted.

The moment arrived for Bawo to make his initial proclamation as king. From the moment he was declared Olu Designate, he knew this moment would be dedicated to honouring his mother. His father had never married his mother and, thus, had never honoured her. He was about to change that. He had discussed this with Amenze, and she agreed with him.

"My mother," he said, "shall no longer be known or addressed in Itsekiri land as Oma Domingo, but she shall be known and addressed as Iye-Olu Erejuwa II." Yes, Oma Domingo was no longer a palace maid but the mother of Olu Erejuwa II and must be addressed as such.

He turned to look at Amenze. Her big, genuine smile and the approval in her eyes meant everything to him.

"My wife–" he paused. He was on the verge of straying from the script. This would surprise Amenze because he had not discussed this part with her. "My wife shall no longer be known or addressed in Itsekiri land as Princess Amenze Sisan Tunoka, but she shall be known and addressed as Olori Erejuwa II."

The king's proclamations were greeted with much cheering from the people. The singers again took centre stage to praise the new king.

Ekun Fifen!

(Holy deity!)

Ogbowuru!

(The one with a great entourage!)

Afomasin!

(The one who says a thing, and no one questions or challenges it!)

Afortse!

(The one who decrees, and it comes to pass!)

Afoweretsewere!

(The one who acts according to what he says!)

Ekun kperegede osun!

(The lion that appears in broad daylight!)

Jenekpo osundada!

(The bright day leopard!)

Our crown, our pride, our unity!

Ogiame! Olu Erejuwa II! The Olu of Warri!

Ruler of the land and sea! Monarch of the universe!

*****

As Bawo lay beside Amenze in bed that night, exhausted and elated, he enquired about her thoughts on his proclamations. Her face lit up with happiness.

"*Ofo re atse ren.* Your word is final." She cradled his face and kissed his forehead.

"*Afomasin.* The one who says a thing, and no one questions or challenges it." She dropped feathery kisses on his eyelids.

"*Afotse.* The one who decrees, and it comes to pass." She kissed both cheeks.

"Ogiame Erejuwa II, the Olu of Warri Kingdom. Monarch of the land and sea. My husband. My pride. *Ogiame suooo.*" She embraced him tightly, locking her lips with his in a lingering kiss.

-THE END-

ABOUT ETURUVIE EREBOR

British by birth and Nigerian by descent, Eturuvie 'Evie' Erebor is an inspirational and self-growth speaker, writer, publisher, talk show host, and lawyer. She has written twenty-two books and published her article series, 'Preparing to Cleave', on the Vanguard Newspaper's Christian page in Nigeria between 2004 and 2007. Her articles have also been published in various newsletters and magazines, as well as on FaithWriters.Com.

Since 2004, she's spoken in churches and schools, transforming the lives of women and youth. Due to personal experience, she's determined to add more value to the lives of her fellow women. Hence, she began her initiative, 'DOZ Network'—writing and publishing DOZ Magazine, DOZ Devotional, and DOZ Chronicles, as well as hosting DOZ Show and DOZ Live Inspirational Conference.

A passionate storyteller, she's currently working on stories that appeal to women who are romantics at heart, and aid in her lifelong mission to educate, inspire, and empower with everything she does.

ABOUT DOZ CHRONICLES

DOZ Magazine was created to publish the stories of women, some painful, some joyful but all inspirational. When DOZ Magazine began operations in 2009, our true stories comprised a section within the magazine. However, readers quickly grew tired of reading the stories piece by piece. They came to loathe the phrase "to be continued", so we created an independent magazine dedicated to telling our inspirational stories in their entirety in a series. This magazine was known as the DOZ (True Story) Magazine, which significantly affected readers. It went out of circulation for a few years, but due to popular demand, it returned in 2015 as DOZ Chronicles. Under this title, four novellas were published, namely, DOZ Chronicles: Kemi, DOZ Chronicles: Lara, DOZ Chronicles: Ruki, and DOZ Chronicles: Nneka. They were published under the African Women Narratives series, and each is based on actual events.

The vision of DOZ Chronicles is expanding with its first fiction novel, DOZ Chronicles: Oloi.